UNLOCKING THE GOLDEN SCROLL

AN ADVENTURE

J W POWELL

Wandering Stream

Literary and Publishing

info@wandering stream.org

COVER BY BRETT GRIMES DESIGN

Statements create debate
Questions open minds
Stories unlock hearts

Other novels by the author

From the Renascence Series:
The Ruction
The Revolution

Acknowledgements

First of all, thank you, Lord for the gift and calling to communicate your Kingdom through storytelling. What a fabulous journey I get to be on.

Also, every writer needs help to make a story readable. Three key players helped me take this adventure to greater levels than I could accomplish alone.

Emily LaCroix is a beloved friend who has a natural feel for visual context. How does a book have visual context, you might ask? When a reader can see what is being read, a scene can be imagined, a character's actions can be grasped; that is visual context. She lets me know when she can and can't see what's going on. She tells me when there is conflict with another part of the story. In addition, she catches the grammar and spelling. Those are precious gifts I appreciate warmly.

My brother-in-love, Jean Rodgers, knows how a story should flow and connect. When great swelling words have inflated beyond the average comprehension, his circles and arrows find me out. When scenes and dialogue over-complicate, he helps me simplify. As an avid reader with an intuitive handle of this craft, he has the liberty to say what is and isn't working. His nuts and bolts comprehension are welcome helps to the mechanics of storytelling.

Ann is my champion; always encouraging and supportive. Writing causes a disconnect on both sides of the computer when a writer's mind is lost in character and scene creation. My wife understands that world and covers my shortfalls with a lot of grace. Thank you so very much for helping me bring these stories to life.

Table of Contents

Introduction 1

Chapter 1 3

Chapter 2 9

Chapter 3 16

Chapter 4 22

Chapter 5 31

Chapter 6 35

Chapter 7 40

Chapter 8 43

Chapter 9 49

Chapter 10 51

Chapter 11 60

Chapter 12 64

Chapter 13 69

Chapter 14 72

Chapter 15 75

Chapter 16 79

Chapter 17 86

Chapter 18 88

Chapter 19 91

Chapter 20 97

Chapter 21 105

Chapter 22 110

Chapter 23 117

Chapter 24 124

Chapter 25 128

Chapter 26 131

Chapter 27 135

Chapter 28 141

Chapter 29 145

Chapter 30 154

Chapter 31 158

Chapter 32 173

Chapter 33 180

Part 2: Fireside Chats

1. A Note from Caleb 190

2. Peeling the Layers 193

3. The Defining Factors 197

4. The Science in Question 206

5. Watch You Languages 213

6. How Do You See It? 217

7. Forming the Scroll 222

8. The Backstory 228

9. Endnotes 232

Introduction by Caleb Hutchins

The mid twenty-first century was dawning in those days and our world view had taken a beat-down. On the one hand, socio-economic manipulators wanted an easy-to-control conciliatory state. On the other hand, dream weavers dreamt about a coming ecotopia that would save the planet. In between those hands, politicians, media mind meddlers, dramatists and opinion mongers wasted little time noising a flatulent narrative that reeked of a hopeless future and stunk with critical self-seeking. All its politic turbulence was a gastronomic power storm at the time. I laugh now at the meaningless drivel at the core of it.

I was a teenager. And in that back-drop of upheaval Bobby Kromberg and I crossed paths. Through the years of adventures, exploits and relentless tribulations that followed, our friendship was forged to a keen edge. The world changed, and we had a big part in it. No — actually, we had a huge part in it. We were conquering warriors, and we overcame the world.

Becoming a world changer wasn't a page in my plan book, but Bobby got that calling when he was a kid. For me, the process was mostly painful and sometimes a lot of fun. In other words, I didn't volunteer because it looked glorious. By the time I was aware of what God was doing, I couldn't say no. I was all in.

Bobby and I survived countless ordeals that led to new breakthroughs for the Kingdom of God. But we understood God was with us and he constantly helped us. Looking back at the crucibles we faced, they prepared us for the work we did. We were set up for success by those difficulties.

But we couldn't pull it off as we did without our encounter with the Golden Scroll. Unlocking all that is powerful from that scroll, is what this story sets up. The scroll of faith and truth became one of the greatest forces behind our message. We used it effectively along with the presence of God's Spirit.

What Papa God started through Bobby and I was brilliant; everything designed in Heaven. Remembering all the steps is still exciting. But I'm too old now to continue zeal like I had back then. With the vision I have now, I understand that I was never meant to finish the work. So, I have passed the torch to other generations who are advancing well. I offer that torch to you if you will accept it. God will show you great and wonderful things if you're hungry for them and have the courage to live them. Although we gained some victories, there are endless victories to be had. Plus, there are enemies at the door waiting for us to let down our guard. We cannot grow complacent.

This story reveals the birthing of the reformation we now experience. It was wrought in the fire of our early days and gained further shape by those who surrendered their lives to God and joined us to give it life.

By reading this story, perhaps you will join us too. Surrender to him, love him passionately and you will not fail at what he gives you to do. And one last thing. No matter what comes, don't be afraid. You will never be alone.

With that, I hand you over to this writer and his craft who made order of the chaos that swirled around me in those days. I tip my hat to him for bringing a resemblance of peace and purpose to it.

And now, God's peace be with you. And may the eyes of your heart understand. — Caleb Hutchin

Chapter One

Bobby Kromberg rose from his chair behind the desk in the den after two hours of intense focus. He stretched then wove his fingers over the top of his blonde curly hair. With homework done for his 'gifted' classes, he felt deserving of some fun. It was Thursday night. On the other side of Friday was a relaxed Saturday with his dad. His thoughts scanned through ideas of what he liked to do. It was too dark to play basketball. A video game wouldn't help him unwind. Read a good mystery; there was something. With that intention, he headed upstairs.

He swiped his notebook screen then laid on his bed. A couple chapters into the story, he stopped to consider the plot. He loved outwitting the endings before they were obvious. His ideal writer hid conclusions well and if he got close to the end and was finding it tough to process, he would stop and dig deeper into the characters. Sleuthing a complicated storyline was a thrill most kids his age never ventured. He closed his eyes to ponder his options.

That's when the room unfolded, slid into the ground and he was left lying on the familiar rock outcrop that overlooked the remote gated valley where he lived. He got up and looked over the ledge. His father's estate was a short distance to the east. That's where he had been reading. His personal observatory stood sixty feet behind it. His Grandma Rachel's place was just below. Everything looked as it should; nothing unusual. Unexpected weird experiences like this were common to Bobby. They could be real. Or it might be a dream or vision. It was hard to tell the difference.

The hoot of an owl cut through the night air behind him and to the right. Moments later feathers brushed across his back, followed by its trailing wing wind. The bird's dark silhouette headed away from him toward thick pine trees on the other side of the valley. He chuckled as he watched his old friend go hunting nocturnal rodents.

He looked up and sighed with wonder. A moonless sky was alive with a hundred million stars in a luminous cloud. Its marvel and mystery stirred tinglings in the nerve clusters of his lower abdomen. The sensation caused him to involuntarily take a step back from the edge of the rock.

"And God said," a familiar voice announced, "Let there be bright lights to shine in space to bathe the earth with their light. Let them serve as signs to separate the day from night and signify the days, seasons, and years."[1]

Bobby turned to the voice and greeted his friend with a hug. The Hunter, who always wore camo-wear and sported a bow with arrows, had appeared on several occasions since Bobby was a toddler. At other times, angels would come instead. There was always time to chat, and sometimes a message or idea to pass on.

"Tonight, Bobby, these stars are a sign." The Hunter made a circle with his thumbs and index fingers and raised it to the southern horizon. He offered Bobby a view through the frame he made. "In just a short while, you will see a sign in this area up close." He lowered his hands and extended a folded paper. "Take this note to your dad."

Bobby opened the note. An expected glow allowed him to read it. The paper showed a time, a date and strings of letters, signs, dashes and numbers he vaguely understood. He refolded the paper and put it in his jean pocket. "What then?"

"Your dad will know what to do.

"Tell the world about the sign that you will see. The greatness and might of it will change the way people live for a time. And then a new season for earth will come. Be courageous, Bobby, and tell them the truth. Those who believe in me, will not be hurt by what will follow."

The Hunter vanished and Bobby was back in his room. He scrambled from bed and put down the notebook. Inside his right-hand pocket was the message written by The Hunter. The handwriting looked like his own. He chuckled and said, "I'm just a twelve-year-old kid . . ."

He touched the screen on his notebook. The time was three thirty-three. His dad got up at four. Bobby saw an opportunity meet with him and have his coffee waiting. As he headed downstairs, the prophet Jeremiah[2] came to mind. He opened a bible on his notepad as he descended the stairs. With plenty of time to make coffee before dad arrived, he looked for 3:33 in Jeremiah. There wasn't one. "Obviously 33:3," he mumbled.

"Call to me," he read, "and I will answer you, and show you great and mighty things, which you do not know."

He signed off, thanked the Spirit for the confirmation, then went through the steps of brewing coffee. As he waited, he leaned against the countertop and studied the note the Hunter had given him.

"You look like you slept in your clothes, Bobby." Richard said as he walked into the kitchen, hair uncombed and wearing pajamas. "Another night with a good book?"

"Not completely," Bobby responded. "I spent part of it on Vision Rock with the Hunter." The Hunter was family code for Jesus. He had been visiting family members; except for Richard; for generations. Richard had a more practical calling.

With raised eyebrows he responded, "Pour me some coffee before you tell me more."

After a couple sips, Bobby showed his dad the note and shared the conversation that went with it.

Richard listened, sipped and read the note. When he looked up, he just had to smile. "This one is really off the charts, Bobby. Fifty astronomical units[3] out in space is a long way. To see space objects clearly will require a special telescope."

"Fifty AUs is four billion miles," Bobby calculated in his head. "The Kuiper Belt."

"There's only two telescopes that see that far with clarity," Richard responded. "To get access to either one of them on a specific night and time like this, may mean we have to share our information so others can be looking in. And they're going to want to know where we got that information. I won't be able to get by telling them that my son's a genius. — Any ideas?"

"I have to tell the truth, Dad. Would it be the first time a science breakthrough happened because someone had a dream?"

"Bobby, this is an event, not a breakthrough," Richard said gentle but firm. "You've given me ideas before that have proven to be workable scientific discoveries. Those breakthroughs were developed without inconveniencing other works in progress. — This is a premonition. It'll be a tougher sell." Then raising a finger he added, "Trust me."

"I'm just the messenger, Dad. The Hunter started it; prayer will finish it. It's not that hard." Bobby smiled and added, "Trust me."

Richard laughed and said, "I do, Son. I'm just one scientist amongst an aggressive and impatient scientific community. I have to face these guys head to head. It's never pretty or easy, and there's always resistance. Even my supporters will balk at this one."

"You're right Dad," Bobby responded nodding his head. "I'm sorry you have to go through that. — What are those other numbers and letters about?"

Richard smiled, realizing his son had gently changed the subject. "Sometimes you're way older and smarter than I give you credit for. — These string notations are celestial references. You've used them on a smaller scale in your own observatory. These are more specific and cover broader details. There's a lot out there and we're looking for a seed in a warehouse. Those coordinates will locate that seed."

The thrill of a new adventure charged the room. Bobby thought of other unforgettable times he shared with his dad. This would be one of them.

Richard got up and poured more coffee, then returned to the kitchen table.

"Dad, have we ever lost anything because of my revelations?"

Richard thought for a moment while looking through the deep blackness in his cup.

"That's an interesting question. I'll grant that our greatest advances have had the toughest resistance. Every advance has had its fights and we shouldn't forget that.

"To answer your question, I've gained some grey hair and lost a lot of sleep. Beyond that, your revelations have added a lot for this family and benefit for others. It seems like we're always moving something forward . . . I guess it's scary and hard work to break new trails, isn't it?"

He looked Bobby in the eye and smiled. "But I couldn't wish for better people to do that with than you and the Lord."

Chapter Two

Three and a half months later.

Bobby and his dad sat in their rented car looking at the walking space between them and the observatory. Oncoming twilight had shifted toward darkness enough to bring on lighting around the parking lot. A small group of people were waiting by the entrance.

They were in the Antofagasta Region of northern Chile. More precisely, the Atacama Desert. The Extremely Large Telescope on Cerro Armazones was classed as a one hundred thirty-foot mirror; making it capable of seeing the cosmic event the Hunter said would take place in the Kuiper Belt beyond the Plutonian orbit.

Tonight, was their night. Richard's connections favored their obtaining this date and time. But not without pushback. Between them and the door was a potential dispute with scientists waiting their turns for time after Richard and Bobby were done.

They left the car and headed for the door. Comments heightened as they approached. So did Richard's reaction to what they said.

Those displaced by Richard's favor had made certain critical word got around. Their disapproval had done its work to gather resistance. Richard reacted accordingly, hurried Bobby inside and locked the door. Agitated and talking with his hands, Richard ranted, "My life would be incredibly easier if I didn't have these skirmishes with the physics community. Did you hear what they said, Bobby? They accused us of *'wasting extremely valuable scientific resource and disrupting more important research.'"* He took a deep breath to quiet his mind. It wasn't easy. He stopped walking and took another breath. "They're just acting the way I expected them to act; they'll want their revenge someday. I don't know why I'm whining about it."

Pointing at Bobby with his index finger, he added calmly, "Don't forget the lesson of tenacity, Bobby; never give up and never surrender to pressure. The struggle to get *this* time on *this* night at an observatory that is capable of seeing what we're about to see is a prime example of how to deal with people who oppose you and the things God has you do. Your great grandpa Jackson, made a lot of money and a good name taking wise risks, being patient and holding his course under the fire of other opinions. Our family learned a lot from the legacy he left behind and I'm glad I got to know him. What he gave me I now give to you."

Bobby shrugged his shoulders calmly and said with a smile, "God answers prayer, Dad. And people hate God for the good he does."

"Bobby, you and Grandma Rachel have the same DNA. You see God in everything."

"Dad, I've been seeing angels since I was a toddler. The invisible world around us is my normal."

"Not to me, Son. God gave me the gift of practical. That's the world around me. But when I get behind a telescope, that's where I *see* God."

"Maybe that's why we make a good team," Bobby rejoined, "because we're different."

"And that's why I trust you, Bobby. What you see and experience in the invisible is always validated with results.

"You're right. We make a good team. The day you go off to college will be a great day for you and a sad day for me. I think that will be the day my life becomes ordinary again and your life will go way beyond anything I could accomplish. I'm looking forward to watching that happen and encouraging you along the way. But I will miss you.

"Okay, enough of that. We have work to do to get everything in place and dialed in. Let's get at it. First thing . . . let's get that lens pointed toward the south east. Here's the controls. Look familiar?"

"It's better quality than mine. But the theory is the same . . . I got it, Dad."

In an hour, the final touches were nearly done.

"We're dialed in on the coordinates and the wavefront," Richard announced while giving the computer monitor the final finger slides and pokes. "The Acumen System will compensate for earth's rotation and manage the adaptive optics from here. For the most part, we're hands free."

He turned and said with a warm smile, "We're ready, Bobby." Then his eyes lit with excitement. "Let's get a look at what's out there."

Richard switched the monitor feed to the nine screens composing the auxiliary theater. They walked through the door and sat in the comfortable chairs directly in front of the screens. Bobby grabbed the remote and turned off the lights while one hundred fifty-seven square feet of deep space unfolded with a quiet blip.

Bobby got out of his chair and moved forward. His crossed arms helped control his excitement. Richard leaned forward with his chin cupped in his hands and elbows on his knees. As Bobby admired the content on the screen, Richard analyzed it.

"I know this is a beautiful thing, Bobby. But tell me what you see. The microphones will pick up and transcribe our conversation." Richard chuckled and added, "We need some chatter;

we're making history. Let's record it."

Bobby understood what his dad was doing. He had worked with him before. Bobby was on an uncertain mission. But Dad wasn't celestial sight-seeing for God while he watched. He was about science, and now was the time for critical analysis and capturing facts. Bobby forced himself to focus his mind and look for details.

"These two guys are ice planets," Bobby said making green circles with his laser pen. "They're more reflective than these three over here. Those are dwarf gas planets. It's hard to say what size they could be, Dad."

"The computer will tell us that, Son." Richard responded as he wrote down his own observations.

"This one," Bobby resumed, "is obviously a rock planet. These three marbles are its moons."

Minutes passed as the spacescape remained unchanged. Then Richard stood abruptly and headed to the right. Pointing with his red laser, he exclaimed, "Look at this, Bobby!"

Bobby followed his dad's movements. At the upper right corner of the screen, an object rolled into the sleeping neighborhood of planets.

"That looks like Saturn's Hyperion moon," Bobby said wide-eyed, "like a banged-up potato. It's a lot bigger and uglier than Hyperion. How fast is it moving?"

"The average is around two thousand miles a minute. You add mass to that speed and impact would be explosive. Add atmosphere to the impact and it gets apocalyptic. In this case, we don't have atmosphere. But with that size and speed, we will have chaos.

"Let's super-impose a line on its trajectory. A few taps on the keyboard — and — done.”

Anticipation heightened; trajectory revealed the aggressor's intent. Richard clicked on the keyboard again. “I'm setting up the system for post-impact tracking. Hopefully we'll get coordinates for all the players involved — or at least the main players.”

An ice planet shattered and the big potato's trajectory changed. After devouring its first victim, the trajectory line recalculated. The rock planet appeared to be next.

“It could slip behind it or go by in front of it, Bobby,” Richard inserted.

Fifteen minutes trudged by in the waiting. The big potato disappeared behind the rock then reemerged.

“They missed!” Bobby yelled.

“No! They collided!” Richard insisted. “Look at the line. Your big potato changed trajectory just a little. Watch this.” Richard tapped the keyboard. Motors whined on the machinery. “I'm pulling back the magnification a notch. It'll give us a bigger picture.”

Bobby watched the screen and shoved his perspiring hands in his pockets. The screen went blank and rebooted. The new position made everything smaller but brought more area into view. A debris field grew behind the rock planet. The big potato had broken and headed toward the edge of the screen. The rock wasn't moving . . . or was it.

“It's coming this way, isn't it?” Bobby asked.

“Sure looks like it.” Richard measured the implications. “Under any other circumstance, the odds of it hitting earth wouldn't be worth the bother to calculate. Where we are in orbit around the sun will change constantly. The asteroid belt between Mars and Jupiter is full of obstructions. The gravitational pull of the sun and a dozen other variables will prevent anything accurate from being perfected at this time. In open space, astrophysicists consider a hundred-thousand-mile pass-by a close call. What we just saw is fifty astronomical units out; four billion miles . . ."

"What do you mean by 'under any other circumstance?'" Bobby interrupted.

"We are here because we were told to come. It will be years before we can have any definitive understanding about what just happened and how it affects us. But we have to ask ourselves: Why were we told? Why us? Why now? Is this thing going to hit Earth?"

"The Hunter said this event would change the way we live," Bobby responded. "He didn't say it would hit us."

"Either way, Son, people will be afraid. Life is scary. How this will plays out will make brave people panic. It won't be pretty.

"Depending on that thing's actual speed, we have ten to fifteen years to make our peace with what *change* will mean."

"Dad," Bobby said soberly. "What about now?"

"What do you mean?"

"You said other people would be looking in, too. You exchanged the coordinates to have the time here."

Richard crossed his arms and rested his eyes on the screen. "So, what you're saying is, we can't stay silent about this."

Bobby raised his hands. "We *have* to tell the world, Dad. We *have* to tell the truth. We *have* to warn them."

Richard shook his head. "It's too volatile! Like I said before, there's only two observatories capable of seeing what we saw tonight. Unless the other one had its eyes focused on it too, the smaller observatories just saw light blips moving in the sky; nothing more. We're pretty safe to wait."

"But we have a record of everything we saw! It's all recorded."

"Relax, Son. We'll forward all the data to the house and put a password on the copy that remains here. Let's wrap it up and head for home."

Bobby saw compromise in what his dad said. "But Dad, the Hunter told me to tell the truth!"

"Bobby, the truth will cause global pandemonium! We're going to wait."

Chapter Three

The bonds between Bobby and his dad unraveled during their return flight from South America. Bobby, seeing a menace hurling through space toward Earth, was convinced that telling the truth meant full disclosure to everyone.

To Richard, the approaching peril needed practical preparations. He saw a bigger, more complex picture. Announcements of that magnitude without careful answers to hard questions would trigger an uncontrollable global reaction. Daily life and governments would spin into chaos.

Bobby saw his responsibility to honor Jesus' instructions. Richard saw his obligation to wait for clearer understanding and counsel. If there *was* a middle ground, they were not finding it. They arrived home in silence.

* * * * * * * * * *

Whistling sweetly, Rachel wandered about the garden watering her flowers and vegetables. She treasured sunny mornings, birdsong and the fragrance of nearby honeysuckle. Along with her whistling and occasional humming, she filled in harmonies to nature's symphony. An approaching shuffle on the dirt path from Vison Rock added familiar percussion to the mix.

"Hi Bobby," she called loudly. "Care to join me for hot chocolate?"

Bobby trod out of the shade of the forest trail, the morning light exposing a gloomy face. His hands and arms were shoved straightly into his pockets and his shoulders were tight.

One of Rachel's cats zoomed across his path to beat him home. But Bobby kicked him instead and sent him tumbling.

"Stupid cat," Bobby moaned. He picked up the stunned kitty and kept walking. "Mister Bojangles, when are you going to learn to get out of the way when someone's coming?"

Rachel detected deeper meaning in his statement. She reached out to take her cat and said, "Mister B will always do cat things. He's just a cat. Of course, when you're not around, he uses his superpowers to keep the squirrels out of my vegetables. It's really quite fascinating to watch."

"No Grandma, he's not Cat Man in sub-human form. He always runs in front of me. I'm sorry, I wasn't paying attention."

Rachel put Mister Bojangles down, straightened up, put her arm around Bobby and guided him toward the kitchen door. "So, what's got you so distracted? Does this have anything to do with your trip to South America?"

"Grandma, there's trouble coming that will affect billions of lives and Dad won't let me warn them! A huge rock is bearing down on this planet that will change the way everybody everywhere will live."

"Oh, my goodness! And how soon will this trouble arrive?" They walked through the door as she waved a hand toward the kitchen table. "Have a seat. This looks like a two-cookie conversation." She took a small platter from the cabinet and added cookies from a ceramic frog.

"Dad said ten to fifteen years, and he says waiting is the best thing to do. But waiting is so unfair, people have to be told. Besides that, the Hunter told me that I was to tell the truth and give the world hope."

Mentioning the Hunter stirred memories. Rachel's parents came to this valley before she was conceived. They were the first ones of her family to meet the Hunter and experience heavenly manifestations. In those days, there was a flock of talking goats that knew the word of God and could heal the sick. Her early life was normal with play times that included the Hunter and the goats.

Her family left this valley to pursue a calling that the Hunter had given her father. His stories kept the valley alive in her by reading them and retelling his experiences. And she never tired of hearing and rereading them.

Jesus, who is the Hunter of lost lives, appeared to her when she was a teenager. He said he would bring her back to the valley as a prayer watcher over the family's eternal inheritance. That day came when she married the grandson of the man who owned the valley. Together, they developed it into large estates. The Hunter chose who would live there; world changers every one of them. That was Bobby's destiny, too. She prayed for him constantly

"That's a weighty message for a twelve-year-old to proclaim. Should I be building an ark, selling my possessions or joining a colonial settlement on Mars to get ready?"

"This is serious, Grandma."

"Yes, it is . . . unless it isn't. It's just that solutions to big problems are hard to find when the weight of them are crushing you. Maybe we need to have a few laughs first."

"Come on, Grandma. You're not making sense."

"Sure I am. Look at Noah and Abraham. Noah built an ark for a hundred and twenty years while raising a family, growing crops and talking with his neighbors about God. Abraham spent a lot of time believing in a promise about a son, managing a huge household and telling his neighbors about God.

"When all was done, God was the central figure in all that happened. Noah and Abraham did what they were supposed to do and God took care of what he was supposed to do. He simply needed faith and obedience from Noah and Abraham to work out the final details."

"What does that have to do with laughing?" Bobby wondered. "What's the point?"

"The point is, they couldn't carry the weight of their callings for all those decades of time. It would have killed them. Sure, they struggled with it. But I believe they learned to give that weight to God, trust him and have time for laughs.

"Neither one could *make* what was going to happen, happen by trying harder and being in control. They had to walk with God during the process and rest in the fact that God was working out his timing."

Rachel let Bobby process . . . "Okay," Bobby said when he was ready. "I get that the rock is going to be here when it gets here. There's nothing I can change about that. But I can change how Dad's handling this; it isn't right. He's standing in the way of letting people prepare."

Rachel thought a few seconds. Another idea came to mind that took a different direction.

"It seems I remember another twelve-year-old that knew he should be about his Father's business. He held all the rabbis in the temple spellbound with his knowledge and wisdom and could have been the greatest twelve-year-old rabbi the world had ever known. But was Jesus called to be a great rabbi?"

"Yes, he was," Bobby responded slowly. "And no he wasn't. He was appointed to be the Messiah — our Savior."

"So, was there something more important at stake? — When his parents found him, what did he do?"

"He resisted at first. And then he went with them."

"And?"

Bobby reviewed the scripture in his mind. His face relaxed and he answered, "He was submissive to his parents."[1]

"He had a choice to make, didn't he?"

Bobby thought . . . "I don't see what his choice was."

"He could *be about his Father's business* — eighteen years prematurely; with who-knows-what kind of results. Or, grow up more and wait for John the Baptist to set up the timing. I'm sure it was a weighty decision."

"Jesus is God. I'm just a boy . . . there's no comparison."

"You feel the fate of the world on your shoulders — as he did. You feel the urgency of Jesus' commission to you — just as the Father's commission must have been urgent words to Jesus. But have you asked Jesus how he wants you to handle what it is he's given you to do? — Now do you see your choices?"

Bobby sighed, "I think so. Break the news to the world on a podcast or blog and do what I think Jesus said to do. Or, submit to my Dad . . . and wait. And when God is ready to tell the world, he'll get the job done.

"It still isn't fair. People will die. Life will be a mess. But I guess there is a choice."

Rachel smiled and nodded her head with understanding. "The steps of the God-pursuing ones follow firmly in the footsteps of the Lord, and God delights in every step they take to follow him.[2] For you, those steps may be tried by fire. When you go back to Vision Rock, ask questions. Ask Jesus for his perspective on this situation. There's more to be revealed that you can't see yet."

Bobby looked like he was taking her words to heart, followed by a sigh of resolve. Then a twinkle appeared in his eye. "Thanks

Grandma. I'll consider your good advice. It would be even better advice if it went with another cookie."

"Now there's my humor . . . now you're ready for that hot chocolate and some fresh ideas about saving the world."

Chapter Four

Eleven years later

Caleb stood with his back to the fire watching the sky from under the bill of his cap. Dawn approached in the treetops. And as the stars dimmed, his anticipation brightened. An half hour before, his hopes for the hunt made it easy to crawl out of his warm sleeping bag and face the mountain country's crisp chill of autumn. He rekindled the fire and set the coffee pot on a rock next to it.

Feeling the warmth of the fire, his dad got up, shook out his boots and put them on. He stretched out his back, looked at the coffee pot then put on his jacket. It wasn't steaming yet, so he asked, "How long?"

Caleb shrugged his lean shoulders and said, "Maybe five minutes."

David wouldn't be talkative until coffee was in him. He groaned quietly and stared at the fire.

Standing close to the glow of the fire in fleece-lined jackets and pants, they waited for sun rise. Caleb smiled and waited for his dad to come alive. Meanwhile, he mentally went through his checklist again. Their compound bows lay in the back of the truck and ready; check. Bottled water and protein bars in their orange vests; check. And then flipping through minor details that were routine from experience, he knew they were ready.

"I've been looking forward to this trip for a long time, Pops,"

Caleb said fidgeting. "First light is almost here."

David poured his coffee, then stood beside him facing the campfire's glow. He sipped the campfire brew then said, "I'm sorry we didn't make it last year, Caleb. I'm so thankful for the chance to make it up to you."

Caleb looked at him annoyed then responded, "That's the third time you've apologized, Dad. You were traveling on construction jobs last year. I understand the cost of responsibility. I get that and I'm over it."

David faced him with a smile. "Thanks for your honesty, Son — Happy sixteenth birthday. This *is* a landmark year for you and I really want this trip to be special."

Caleb wasn't one to rehash the past. He returned his dad's gaze and said, "It already is, Pop."

Caleb's words warmed David's heart more than the mug warmed his hands. He was starkly aware that Caleb was almost as tall as himself. The years were getting shorter and Caleb's manhood was just beginning.

Letting his son down pointed to a deep conviction. Growing up without a dad made his family commitments more than simply caring. He wanted his only son to know he would always be there for him. Guilt crept in when his promises were left unfulfilled. Caleb didn't know, but he had to threaten to quit his job if he didn't get the time off to be on this hunt. He questioned how responsible that manipulative maneuver was.

Caleb grabbed his shoulder unexpectedly. "Dad, there's something going on! Look at the sky."

The cobalt blue of the forest dome lightened to ultramarine then azure. A brilliance as radiant as day exploded then went out like a shattered light bulb. The event left the two looking at each other. Seconds later a thunderous concussion rippled through the trees and brushed across their faces.

"Whoa! That was freaky. — Whatever it was probably spooked every deer in these mountains."

Disappointment marked Caleb's face. A fatherly hand went across his shoulder in response. "We have the whole week if we need it. We'll just have to be patient. Remember, it ain't over 'til it's over."

From the distance, thuds pounding the ground and the cracks of limbs snapping started.

"Listen to that Caleb! It sounds like a stampede heading toward us."

Heavier wallops pounded like the footfalls of a running giant. A noise like wooden mallets striking face to face added a foreboding tension. A sudden, furious din began in the distance and rumbled toward them. Then the large part of a tree fell.

"Get covered!" David yelled.

Caleb looked for a log. There wasn't any. Confused, he hesitated.

David tackled him, falling on top to protect him. A treetop above them exploded, raining splinters and chunks. Rocks hammered the ground.

David raised up, then went limp. Chaotic noise increased to a roar then quickly moved away from them, leaving the running giant to slow his pace then stop.

Warm liquid dripped on Caleb's neck. "Dad?" There was no response. "Dad!" Caleb yelled.

He pushed up and squirmed from under him. "Dad!" Caleb rolled him over to check him by the firelight. His head was bleeding badly. "Oh Dad, what do I do?" He stopped to observe; he was breathing. "Come on Caleb, remember Dad's training."

He thought through his survival instructions. "Okay, stay calm in emergencies and respond, don't react."

He took deep breaths and forced himself to get still. He ran to the tent. It lay crumpled and flat with a football-sized rock on it. He pulled up the flap, grabbed a t-shirt, a bottle of water and ran back. Unscrewing the cap, he soaked a part of the shirt.

He looked around, listened for any kind of noise then hollered, "Is anybody out there? I need help. Can somebody hear me?"

A voice in the distance rang back. "Yeah, I'm here. Keep talking. I can't tell where you are."

Caleb knelt, folded the shirt, put it on the wound and poured more water over it. "Jesus, help me," he prayed, then raised his voice again and yelled, "Can you hear me?"

"Yeah I hear you, keep it up."

Caleb called several times; responses grew louder. "I see your campfire. I'll be right there."

Caleb poured water on the wound and wiped gently. Blood flowed, his dad's flesh was gnarled and raw. Some skin was gone. He shivered involuntarily and groaned, "That's not good."

Caleb heard the crunch of branches and looked up as a man in camouflage clothing walked into the light. He had a recurve bow across his shoulder and arrows in his quiver. He looked his dad's age and had a confident bearing. He assessed the situation before speaking.

"Wow, that looks messy," the hunter stated as if it was something he could handle. He removed his archery tools and asked, "What do you think?"

The man's demeanor quieted Caleb's tension.

"The skin is pretty beat up. It's hard to look at without wanting to gag. I really don't know what to do for him, mister. It looks serious, but I can't tell if he's going to be alright."

"You're doing fine. I heard you calling for Jesus. Do you believe in prayer?"

"Yeah. But I'm surprised you heard me. I didn't say it that loud."

"Sound carries far in these woods. That's why the critters always know we're here. Let's pray for your dad's healing. What do you say?"

Caleb felt relieved and said, "Yeah, Jesus can do that."

"You pray, and I'll agree with you."

After they prayed, the hunter asked, "Would you mind a second opinion?"

"No — no, go ahead."

He knelt and pulled back the t-shirt. "It looks like a glancing blow. The skin roughed up pretty bad. He's just knocked out. We'll have to wait till he wakes up before we know how he's doing for sure.

"Tell you what, its light enough. Let's look for something to make a poultice. I saw some stuff near here yesterday that'll work. We can stop any infection and prevent some scarring— But first, pour more water on the wound, then put the t-shirt back on it." Caleb responded with action. "Yeah, just like that. And now, you can help me."

Caleb looked at him with concern.

"It won't take us long," the hunter comforted. "He'll be fine while we're gone."

Away from the campfire, it was easier to see. The meteor's devastating rain shattered and limbed trees, and left a littered landscape of assorted rocks. Caleb felt relieved they weren't killed.

"What I'm looking for," the hunter stated, "is near a boulder that looks like an eagle's head."

Caleb looked around, spotted it and pointed out the silhouette. "Over there."

The hunter searched intentionally. Stooping to pick leaves, bending over to uproot a whole plant or grasp a few flowers. He then handed it all to Caleb. He dug up some bulbous roots and handed them to him also.

He smiled and said, "Those plants and some charcoal from the fire will do it. Let's head back."

When Caleb turned around, a dull shine on the forest floor caught his attention. "What's that?" He stopped, then squatted to inspect it.

Peering from over his shoulder the hunter chuckled and said, "Now *that* looks interesting."

Something tubular and metallic was partially exposed in an oblong rock about two feet in length. "It looks heavy," the hunter added.

Caleb pushed the rock. "It's still hot."

The hunter squatted, touched it and said, "But not too hot to carry." He picked it up with little effort, "Let's get back to your Dad and patch him up. You can explore this guy later."

As camp came into sight, David was sitting up and holding the bloody t-shirt. He was looking around confused and concerned. Hearing crunchy steps over twigs and leaves, he turned his head. He tried to get up, steadied himself with a hand to the dirt then changed his mind.

"If you could get me another bottle of water and find something to heat it up with," the hunter said to Caleb as he put the rock on the ground, "I could get this poultice brewing."

"Do you think I need a doctor?" David asked.

"Since you can talk to me, I'd say you'll be bright as a new star by evening . . . Besides, you and your son have bucks out there with your names on them. I wouldn't let a little meteor shower rush you off."

David looked doubtful. "You believe those bucks will still be around after all this racket?"

"Well, *I'm* sure planning on it," the hunter stated with confidence as he took a sauce pan and water from Caleb when he returned.

"My name is David, by the way. And this is Caleb."

The hunter shook hands with them both and said, "A pleasure to meet you guys under any circumstance. I'll let Caleb tell you about what we found out there . . . And if you'll hand me that t-shirt, I can make a pouch for this mixture and get it on your head." Using a knife from his belt, he cut strips from the clean part of it.

Caleb picked up the rock and sat next to his Dad.

Pointing, he showed the details. "There's this little metal ball and part of a tube sticking out of it. But there's a lot more of it inside. I think it's cooled a little since we found it. It was part of that meteor." Caleb handed it to his dad, went to the truck and brought back the tire iron. He took back the rock and whacked it, breaking off a small chunk.

David grimaced and held out his hands. "Uh, Caleb, let's wait on that. The noise is too . . ."

"Sure, Dad. . . Sorry." He set the tire iron aside. "It'll take some time to break this thing out of here anyway."

"Yeah, son, it certainly looks intriguing. But the noise will scare off any wildlife that's left out here. You want to hunt or break rocks?"

Caleb laughed and said, "I can break rocks anytime. Let's hunt."

The hunter leaned toward the hot embers of the morning fire and stirred the goo he concocted. "Make sure you save the rock you break off. It'll have scientific value."

"Yeah, that's a good idea," Caleb responded.

The hunter stood, set the pan on the ground and let the poultice cool just briefly. Then he dipped a cloth strip in it, folded it, then applied it to David's head, causing a grimace.

"It'll sting for a just a minute — you'll get used to it."

After the initial shock, David relaxed. The hunter wrapped more strips about his head to hold it on. Then he looked at Caleb and smiled. "You'll want to wash out that pan before you do any cooking with it. The flavor is quite disagreeable."

"Thanks for your help, mister . . ." David let the statement dangle to get a response.

"I'm glad I was around to help." He stepped back and added, "You guys will be fine. And now I need to get going; there's hunting to be done. You'll have an adventure story to tell for years to come."

He shook hands with them, got up and put on his bow and

quiver. Heading back the direction he had come, he stopped and turned to ask, "We *did* have quite an adventure, didn't we? . . . I'm sure we'll meet again."

Caleb and David watched as the hunter laughed, turned and walked away. Caleb looked at the bandage and asked, "How you feeling, Dad?"

"I'd feel better if we had gotten that man's name."

"He wouldn't mention it, Dad . . . Why did he do that?"

"Why don't you go after him and be insistent. Get a phone number or something. He needs to be properly thanked."

Caleb went carefully in the direction of where the hunter had gone, shuffling to avoid tripping over debris.

"Hey mister, wait up."

He called repeatedly as he ventured cautiously in. With no responses to his calls, he stopped moving and listened.

The forest was silent.

Chapter Five

Earthly debris and cosmic rock forced cautious movements during their afternoon hunt. In spite of it, Caleb managed a four-point buck after his dad yielded first shot to him. Their reward was the satisfaction of lugging their prize back to the truck.

But back at camp, Dad had a concern. "Son, I will feel safer tomorrow if your mind is properly focused on hunting. I want you more alert than you were this afternoon."

Caleb understood and laughed, "Aliens took me captive, Pops! I couldn't get my mind off that rock. There's something from another world inside that cylinder." Caleb raised a finger for emphasis. "I think it came through a worm hole and it's been drifting in space for thousands of years. And now, I've found it. — Come on, you can't tell me you haven't been wondering."

"Sure I have. But there's logical explanations for these things, Son. It's your head that's in another world. You're not going to find life forms inside of that cylinder."

"Maybe not," Caleb chuckled. "But I hear a mystery in there screaming at the top of its lungs. And I'm the only one listening."

"No, you're not, Caleb. Metal objects falling out of the sky wrapped in space boulder . . . that's a hard scream for me to ignore. I have to admit that I'm intrigued. But . . . more importantly, I'm here to hunt . . . with you. And we've been looking forward to this for weeks. Let's not mess it up by scaring the animals off with a lot of unnecessary noise."

"You mean, I can't work on it tonight? I've been thinking about it all day."

"You can . . . if you can use your superpowers to melt the rock off by staring at it. Listen, we've got all the tools we need at home. It'll be easy work when we get back." David put his hands on his hips and sighed. "It's not going to happen tonight."

Caleb's excitement leaked out of him. With knees bent and head back he moaned, "Come on . . . Really?"

"Caleb, I have to be firm on this. How long have you been hunting with me?"

"Since I was eight years old."

David stared at him silently with raised eyebrows; waiting.

"I know, I know, 'A peaceful hunter creates a quiet environment to attract natural grazing' . . . What rule number is that?"

David put a firm hand on Caleb's shoulder. "This isn't about rules, Caleb."

"Sorry, Dad. I'm being a jerk. We're here to be with each other, and I'm distracted."

"That's right — Don't take me wrong, Son. We'll get excited about space rocks together. Just not now. We're hunting."

Caleb laughed and looked at him squinty-eyed and sideways. "You gotta admit, Dad, this ain't an ordinary hunt."

"Caleb, this is an extraordinary hunt with all that's happened. I'll never forget it. But we came here to reconnect; let's do that. This is our time together. Even this crazy knock on my head feels better. I'm tempted to take the bandage off and see what's happened."

"It looked pretty nasty, Pops. You should be seeing a doctor for a skin graft. Not out here hunting."

David chuckled and removed the rags holding the poultice. "That statement just reeks of an agenda, Caleb."

Caleb looked puzzled.

"What's the matter? Is it infected?"

Caleb took the rags and wet a clean spot from his water bottle and wiped the poultice from his dad's forehead.

"There's no pain," David remarked with a smile.

Caleb found another clean spot on the rag, watered it and wiped it again. He looked from the spot to his dad's eyes, then back again. "You need to look in the mirror, Dad."

David felt the wounded area, got wide-eyed and ran to the truck.

"It's gone!" David turned to stand in front of Caleb. "Touch it, Caleb."

Caleb delicately brushed his fingers over the spot.

"Push on it."

Caleb touched it firmly with one finger.

"Harder," David persisted.

Using three fingers, Caleb pushed him back against the truck door.

"There's no pain, Caleb."

"And no scar," Caleb added. "Just a white spot."

David stared at the forest as if it were enchanted. "That's quite a poultice."

Chapter Six

Caleb handed his mom a safety shield. She took it and said, "Why yellow?" before slipping on the full-face cover.

"It turns your beautiful blue eyes a stunning shade of brown, Layla." David answered instead of Caleb.

Layla looked at David oddly and responded, "That's annoying. Here, trade me. I like the clear one better. . . Did you suffer brain damage or something?"

"Not at all. We left two bucks at the butchers, had a great adventure, survived a potential nightmare and got home early . . . I'm just happy. Happy to be back and alive."

"It's a good thing I wasn't paying attention to the news. I would have been insane with worry." Layla paused trying to muster some anger. Failing, she stated, "You guys should have called."

"You have any idea how beautiful you look with that yellow face shield?" David jibed. "You wanna trade back?"

"Don't push it, Mister Endearment. It's a good thing I missed you or I'd give you a fist pump where it hurts."

David smiled and Layla was done with her rant.

"Mom," Caleb stated knowingly. "Yellow lenses are for low light conditions. Some hunters wear them on overcast days to see movement better."

"Thanks Caleb," Layla responded. "At least I got a straight

answer from *you*."

David reacted with a blown kiss from behind his shield. Layla appreciated it more than she let on and returned a brief smile.

Caleb and David had been in the garage during the late afternoon slowly removing rock at the workbench. Layla had just gotten home from work. "These rock chips tend to scatter," Caleb told her, "and they're as sharp as razors. Stand behind me, it'll give you extra protection."

Layla put her right hand on Caleb's shoulder and her left hand leaned on the workbench. Their story behind the find *was* a marvel. Curiosity radiated at the work bench and filled the air. David held the rock with heavy gloves and turned it while Caleb chiseled pieces of varying sizes off the body.

Layla probed for more detail. "So that hunter guy helped you find this, eh?"

"Yeah, Mom." Caleb looked at David and added, "But there's no question in *my* mind that the *guy* that helped us was an angel. Like I said on the phone, he disappeared right after leaving the camp site."

"I'm not so sure about that," David said. "There was enough time for him to get out of sight."

"But not enough time to get out of earshot," Caleb argued. He turned and added, "I yelled loud, Mom. He didn't respond and there wasn't a noise to be heard anywhere."

"I know how loud you can yell, Caleb," Layla responded with a chuckle. "I've been listening to it for quite a few years. And I'm sure he heard you. He just had good reason for keeping quiet."

"That doesn't make sense. His poultice thing was an excuse to take me to this rock. He knew it was there. . . I can tell."

"Son," David said, "this thing is messing with your reasoning."

"Reasoning?" Caleb pushed back. "How do you *reason* the blood on your clothes and the fact that the injury that caused all that blood . . . is now gone and healed?"

David sighed and shrugged his shoulders. "I can't explain that."

"Give your son some credit, David. Do you suppose . . . us standing in front of a rock from space with a metal object of unknown origins protruding from it, just might be something providential?"

"This rock," David said skeptically, "could have been there before the meteor shower."

"Dad," Caleb said impatiently, "the rock was hot when we found it."

"You're right, Son. I remember now. My head was spinning when you brought it in."

"I hear," Layla teased, "getting struck by moon rock creates confusion."

David laughed and responded googly-eyed, "That's why they call it moonstruck . . . Okay, your point is well taken. Let's peel off this inter-stellar space ship and face what life lurks within."

When done, a mostly round tube emerged about eighteen inches long and five inches in diameter. It had two opposing handles ten inches in length. Inside the handle faces were independent three-pronged forks with single legs attached at one end. Each prong of each fork was a different length.

The ends of the tubes had different purposes. One end was flat so the cylinder could stand. The other end was domed with a ball at the top. Everything about it was simply crafted. Yet, even while roughly removing the rock, it did not crack, scratch or ding. It appeared to be molded as one piece without seam or joint or holes. Although plain, the workmanship was precise.

Caleb took more pictures to cover the before and after, then tried several ways to open it. He twisted counter-clockwise and clockwise. They pulled the ends without twisting; then twisting. They used pipe wrenches, and hit the device around the raised ends with a ball peen hammer . . . Nothing prevailed.

"Anyone for tea?" Layla asked in frustration. "It's time for a break and it's getting late."

"I'll have a beer," David responded.

"I'll take a root beer, Mom."

The cylinder stood as the center-piece at the kitchen table. Thinking and sipping filled the minutes.

"We should give this thing a name," Caleb stated.

David smiled mischievously and asked, "Is it a girl or a boy?"

Layla blinked long and shook her head. "How about something scientific or historical?"

"It has to be unique," Caleb responded.

Minutes ticked by without inspiration.

"I was told at work that Doctor Anika Roos is back in the country." Layla said, moving on.

"I remember her." David said. "Your college roommate. She's popped in on occasion since then."

"Yeah, and she's well connected. — Maybe she would do an old friend a favor and take a look at it."

Caleb objected. "Mom . . . Dad and I talked about keeping this a secret unless it's absolutely necessary to tell someone. If we let the science people get a hold of it, they'll shove me aside and I'll never see it again."

Layla considered his concern and nodded. "Losing contact with it is a real possibility. We would have to be smart about bringing in an expert. Non-disclosure stuff — secrecy, people we trust and all that."

"Complicated comes to mind," David said. "I have seen it happen. An unusual discovery becomes an occasion for those who want to own it and others who just want to be seen with it. All the unethical and political worms come out of the woodwork to be in the spotlight. Everything we do from here will have to be documented and carefully thought out."

"How about," Caleb said with an insistent sigh, "I put it on my bookshelf and we don't tell anybody."

"Caleb," Layla rejoined. "This wasn't handed to you to be put on a shelf and be forgotten. Everything points to a bigger purpose.

"Layla," David responded, "would Anika come out here without needing a reason why?"

"Just to see me? — Not likely. We were school chums on the same path at the time. We've got our own lives now and we're not that close anymore. I think she'd need a good reason."

"I think you should get a hold of her," David suggested. "Cautiously."

Chapter Seven

The glass door of the pellet stove provided little glow compared with the mid-afternoon sun streaming through the nearby windows. But the radiant warmth from the stove was prepared to make any conversation cozy. It was the fifth day of Layla's four-day work week and Layla had settled Anika into her guest room. Then she moved two overstuffed chairs closer to the stove. When Anika arrived in the family room Layla was seated, fresh tea brewed on the stove top and a tray of mugs with cream and sugar waited on the hearth.

Anika nestled into a chair and curled her legs under her. After questions about Anika's comforts and needs, Layla was satisfied with her hosting and ready to focus on rediscovering their friendship.

"I was surprised to hear from you, Anika," Layla stated. "David and I had just talked about getting in touch with you. Then oddly, you call."

"It's not so very odd, really." Anika responded. "I had to call on your boss anyway, so you naturally came to mind. I really wanted some time with you. And you were so nice to invite me to this sweet place of yours while I was here." Anika sighed and continued. "You have no idea what a peaceful change it is to visit a homebody with roots and stability from time to time. I'm such a little wanderer. And most of my colleagues are wanderers, too.

"I keep a small home because I'm never there very long. And I have a live-in caretaker, or it would simply become a mess. How's that for a lifestyle?"

"Well, you're still trim and beautiful, Anika. Archaeology keeps you young and feminine."

Anika looked at her short fingernails. "Honestly, Layla. The only reason I wear fingernail polish is to hide the dirt under my nails. And I haven't given up on finding a man who will follow me around to all my digs. So, I keep doing the work and hope for the best."

"Seeing anyone?"

Anika sighed with a smile. "If I could sit still long enough to be found by someone intelligent, good looking and rich, I would have better luck. But it seems my passions keep me on a constant mission around this planet . . . and unavailable."

"I'll take that as a no. Maybe someday you'll want a home with a companion?"

"Oh Layla. Don't take me wrong. My digs are my home and their relics my lovers. They *are* my passion in the truest sense. I would do *anything* for them."

"Although I heard stories like yours when we were in college, the reality of them are beyond my comprehension. Family is *my* everything. I can't even imagine something taking their place."

"Just remember, Layla dear, you influenced my choice of career path."

Layla tilted her head slightly. "Ah yes, I remember. I'll take some responsibility for that. And with it, I wish you all the best in your career. I'm not sorry I chose the wonderful marvels of family instead of that."

"Sure, family has its rewards and challenges, too. But I have few regrets. Beyond the occasional boredom, I made a good choice and I have considerably more adventures than most ordinary people. In fact, I would call my life extraordinary; you should be jealous."

They giggled as Layla stood and poured the tea.

"Speaking of adventure," Layla confided as she passed the mug to Anika.

"Let me guess," Anika interrupted. "This isn't British tea."

They laughed again as Layla added, "So sorry, I forgot you spent a lot of time in England. You must be spoiled."

"I've learned to survive outside the UK," Anika rejoined and faked a British accent. "I'll add the cream and sugar, if you would please, and I'll be right as rain."

Layla picked up the tray and held it while anika mixed her tea, stirred it and took a sip. "Hmmmm, cheers." Then she continued with a sly smile. "And what could be on your mind?"

Layla replaced the tray to the hearth while answering. "Well, Caleb and David found something when they were in the mountains hunting."

"Intriguing," Anika eagerly barked. "Coming from you, it's got to be good. When do I get to see it?"

"After the guys get home. Caleb's at school and David is working. When we have dinner, I'll turn them loose to tell their story."

"I will look forward to it. If it's okay with you, then, may I have a little time for a shower and a power nap? I *am* a tad off your time zone."

"Sure. I'll knock on your door if I don't see you by then."

Chapter Eight

Unfamiliarity formed by years of distance faded as supper at the kitchen table progressed. Caleb was a small child during Anika's last visit. He felt comfortable with her personal attention, stories of digs, history and technology. They were vivid and captivating. While his mom and dad simply took the narrative as Anika's passion for her craft, Caleb imagined himself in her place solving ancient mysteries. It didn't go unnoticed by Anika.

"I have a funded internship for young people who can volunteer to help with these amazing discoveries. The fund will pay all of your expenses for six weeks during the summer. — Caleb, I'm inviting you to join me. It's an opportunity to see archaeology up close and meet young people from all over the world."

David smiled and raised his eyebrows at the possibility, but Layla balked. "Anika, he's only sixteen and he's never been away from us that long. Sure, a few weeks in the summer at grandpa's house. But, out of the country? Alone?"

"Mom," Caleb objected, "come on!"

Anika put her hand on Layla's. "Layla dear," she pleaded, "when we were in college, these opportunities were special and rare. I'm sure you remember."

"I do. It was one of those opportunities that got us committed to what we do," Layla responded. "But we were twenty and twenty-one. There's a huge difference. We had experience about being on our own. There's a lot of life to deal with out there that Caleb is not ready for."

"I know, dear. But times have changed. Educators see advantages of early stimulation and are willing to put opportunity where their convictions are. They know there are potential pitfalls involved and they have put safeguards in place. There will be parents there as well."

"Mom, please, I want to go." Caleb begged.

"I need to think about it."

"Here's another option," Anika stated. "One of you come along and make it a family experience."

"I'd have to get the time off," David said reluctantly, but then made a leap. "But it would be worth it."

"You'd have to pay your own expenses," Anika added. "It's only fair I tell you."

Shocked, Layla leaned toward David. "You'd make that kind of sacrifice?"

David took a deep breath. "It's scary to think about taking six weeks off. But, I'm willing." Both understood the implications of gain and loss without saying it. They could afford the trip. But David's position as a construction supervisor could be lost.

"This is exciting!" Anika squealed. "You won't regret it. It's a once-in-a-lifetime opportunity. And we will have so much fun. You'll meet people from all over the world. — Oh, I already said that. —You'll have to get a passport."

"This is just a discussion," Layla reminded. "Not a decision."

"Oh dear," Anika sighed. "I've done it again. My zeal has over-taken my sensibilities. Of course, you will have time to make that decision. But you *must* make application before the end of this year to be considered for the internship. Of course, with my vote the committee would go along."

Anika sighed again to calm down. "Speaking of exciting. — I

understand you gentlemen have a story of your own to tell."

"Caleb," David stated, "your version would be more complete. You start."

Caleb grew nervous. He thought the truth was too unbelievable for an experienced treasure finder like Anika. Fidgeting because of his doubts, he started with the planning stage before the trip to ease into it.

"If you will, Caleb," Anika interrupted, "start from when you were in the mountains."

"We were standing at the campfire . . ." Caleb now tried to make his story short, and wrongly perceived a look that told him he was still saying too much. He left out more than he wanted. And when finished, Anika asked questions to clarify details. Then she was silent.

"It's a sincere story; extraordinary even. People who didn't know you wouldn't believe it, but I do. Did you happen to get some pictures of the cylinder while it was still in the rock?"

Caleb pulled out his phone, opened the photos file and handed it to her. "From beginning to end, I took pictures until it was out of the rock."

Anika studied the photos; internally processing through a vast knowledge of history and culture. Unusual facial expressions mirrored a variety of thoughts. When she lay the phone down, she stated, "I've *never* seen anything its equal. It's neither ancient nor modern. It's so plain and ordinary that nothing about it would characterize a particular civilization, or even an era. Perhaps a closer look would be helpful . . . Would you all grant me the honor of a first-hand inspection of this cylinder?"

David and Layla looked each other, then to Caleb. "It's your call, Caleb." David declared. "You're the official finder."

Caleb hesitated. "I guess there's no turning back, now." Caleb got up and left the room. He returned with the cylinder wrapped in a towel. Anika moved dishes and glasses to make room for the cylinder. Caleb unwrapped it and stood it in front of her.

Anika studied and turned it, then studied some more. She got up from the table and opened the kitchen drawers. Pulling out a metal hammer; the small kind with screw drivers in the handle; she returned to the table. She looked at all the faces with childish eagerness. "This is going to be fun."

"Let's do an experiment. These prongs inside the handles are unusual, but they've been around for centuries. Do you know what a tuning fork is?"

"When I was in grade school, I used one to tune my violin," Layla responded.

"Precisely," Anika responded pointing the hammer at her. "I've never seen a three-pronged tuning fork or one that had uneven tines. But I just *have* to know if this little hunch of mine has any merit."

She hit one prong with the hammer. It produced a long, ringing note. Anika smiled, then shivered involuntarily. "Oh my, spine tingling."

Hitting another tine produced a different pitch. Turning to the opposite handle, she did the same thing. "They're all different."

She put the hammer down, placed her elbows on the table and her hands beneath her chin, thinking. When she sat back, she stated, "The tones are the key to opening this cylinder, like a combination to a safe. The question now is: What is the right combination?"

Caleb laughed and professed, "If we do it wrong, we'll get taken to another dimension of time and space."

"So long as we're back for work tomorrow," David said straight faced. "I'm game."

Anika chuckled, took a deep breath and taking aim she quickly tapped three prongs on one side from tall to short. The result was a harmonious ring with an unusual bamboo-like timbre. The volume sustained then increased; the cylinder vibrated.

Fifteen seconds passed, the notes faded and nothing happened.

"Let's remove everything from the table."

"What does that do?"

"Good question, Caleb. A tuning fork works better when using a wooden chamber or surface to amplify the sound. We are going to use this table as a sound board to amplify these forks."

Anika smiled triumphantly and raised her eyebrows. "Grab that butter knife Caleb."

"This time, you strike the three prongs on that side. And I will strike them on this side. At my count, we will hit them at the same time. — One, two, three."

The result was harmonic resonance that went through the table and into the wood floor. The intoned collection moved, altered then included the walls and ceiling. Multiple harmonies emerged then swelled in numbers. It was now an orchestra and growing. The air around them shifted density. Sparkling notes twinkled and faded; new ones of different pitch replaced them. Complimentary melodies emerged as circle-like sounds weaving together. The sparkling melodies concentrated their song toward the cylinder, creating a glowing mist that engulfed it, then filled the room.

"I hear echoes," Caleb sang, trying to match what notes he could. "Hey, this is like singing in a canyon. — Try it!"

Layla overcame her astonishment to join Caleb. David joined in self-consciously. Anika watched. Their hearts raced. They sang louder. Anticipation rose. David yelled a cowboy yeehaw. The others continued a stream of jumbled song until the mist slowly melted away. And yet, the atmosphere remained charged.

Layla and Anika's eyes met.

"Wow," David exhaled.

Caleb exclaimed, "Let's do that again!" and looked at the table. "Hey, what happened to the cylinder?"

Chapter Nine

"Caleb!" Anika commanded. "Take pictures. Get a record of this."

The cylinder lay in pieces and amongst its debris was a rolled-up scroll on a single baton.

Anika spread Caleb's towel and gently removed the cylinder pieces to one end; the scroll to the other. The loose end of the scroll unfurled to reveal unfamiliar characters. She sat back, crossed one arm and cupped her chin with the other hand.

"I don't recognize the symbols. — And the material . . ." She leaned forward and pushed the scroll open with the hammer. "It's not a paper or animal skin; it looks more like linen. The baton looks like a golden stick; like petrified wood."

"Is it gold?" Caleb asked reaching to touch it.

Anika waived him off saying, "Your skin oils could damage it.

"Caleb, a fabric of pure gold with this fine of a weave has *never* been achieved. *Never*. . . And to write on it — would require the wisdom of Solomon." She leaned back and added, "I know of only one person who can shed light on this. To see him, we must go to England."

"No!" Layla shrieked. "What responsible mother would send her sixteen-year-old son to another country with something like this without safeguards in place. Who? I can't let that happen."

"I understand, Layla," Anika responded. "That *is* a lot to ask. — He doesn't have to go. I can . . ."

Caleb interrupted strongly. "You're not leaving me out of this! And this thing is not leaving my sight. I was chosen to protect and preserve whatever this is by whoever delivered it. I want to know who that is and I have to know why. Wherever this scroll goes, *I* go."

"I'm behind you on that, Son." David declared.

"David, you can't allow it!" Layla's eyes welled up and pleaded. "You have to support me."

David understood Layla's heart. She's a mom; protective and sensitive. But in light of what just happened, he was seeing a bigger picture. "Layla, given everything that has happened until now, isn't it obvious that someone wiser than us has planned this?"

"Everything in me is screaming *dangerous,* no matter who planned it. How in the world can I give my approval?"

"Mom, I can do this. I *have* to do this. The only other choice is to not do it at all."

Chapter Ten

Six weeks later at Oriel College
Oxford University in England

Caleb felt the weight of unfamiliar surroundings. British tradition, scholastic excellence and global influence was on unrivaled display throughout the halls and courtyards of Oxford University. A thousand years of artistic and sculptural representation kept record of those hailed as masters of thought, literature and progress. It was a peculiar anointing. All of it generated an energy Caleb had never experienced.

For two days, Anika gave a tour of various Oxford campuses. There were warm welcomes from some, snooty distance from others and inquisitive looks by the rest that confused him. Some were curious because of his age. A few curious why he didn't bow his knee to their greatness. It was easy to make assumptions. The constant attention grew tiresome. Avoiding eye contact, unless forced to acknowledge persistent friendliness, proved helpful. And now it was time for their appointment at Ariel College.

"All these people are world changers, Anika. I should be wearing a sign that says, 'I'm an idiot.'"

"Don't let a thousand years of academic drivel intimidate you, Caleb." Anika chuckled and continued, "One thing I've concluded; all of us die in the end, even if our work continues to have impact after we're gone. The importance of it is a mystery to me. And yet, my work gives me purpose. Somewhere in the great scheme of things is a conspiracy to keep us entertained with ourselves: a divine comedy perhaps.

"Apart from that, highly educated people can be amazingly normal. A few have redefined normal to mean 'outside the box.' It's a by-product of learning to think for yourself and be a leader. Any institution like this would teach you that. I think education simply gives one tools to explore life in all its diversity."

Anika stopped walking and looked Caleb squarely. "Besides, what makes you think *you're* not a world changer? You have as much potential as anyone here."

Caleb shrugged and said, "This is a different planet. I can change my sox. But changing the world? — Come on, that's a special kind of person."

"You're just out of your element, Caleb. Wait till you get used to it. You'll see things differently.

"With that thought," Anika stated as they resumed their walk, "let me give you a heads up about Professor Sholom. He's a down-to-earth gentleman and a rather normal Brit. Although, he is highly prejudicial when it comes to tea and referring to America as *the colonies*. In that respect, he seems stuck in time. You will see that for yourself in short order.

"Don't take me wrongly, I love the UK and Professor Sholom. They're both refreshing changes from Americana. But brace yourself to hear strong opinions and see odd habits."

Anika and Caleb were merely moments late for their appointment. A young man at the reception desk smiled at Anika and asked their purpose. After Anika replied, he nodded politely then ushered them into a spacious office. Caleb spotted several diplomas on the wall, then a man he guessed to be in his fifties rose from behind his desk and hugged Anika. A younger man sat nearby, but stood after they walked in. He smiled at Caleb and nodded.

"My dear Anika, it has been far too long," he said kindly. "It's so good of you to leave your dirt piles and come visit me."

"You have no idea, Professor," she responded warmly. "I love my dirt piles, especially if ancient mysteries are hiding in them. Leaving them is like . . . it's like leaving the comforts of home where I can curl up with personal adventures in a time machine."

"I feel the same way when I travel. It is a cold world out there, and so warm and fuzzy in our beloved institution. I fear I am hopelessly acculturated."

Anika turned to Caleb, "He means, he is lost without this tribe."

"Oh, I am indeed. — Please, forgive me, I am being rude . . . allow me to introduce my young protégé. This is Bobby Kromberg. I am mentoring his PhD thesis. He is from the colonies as well.

"And Bobby, may I introduce to you a *former* protégé of mine, Doctor Anika Roos. She is now a *very* accomplished archaeologist and lover of antiquities."

With a large desk and Caleb between them, Bobby simply nodded and said, "It's a pleasure to meet you, Doctor. I have read your articles about the digs in South America. And I believe you were there when I was there with my father some years ago."

"Then, you would be Doctor Richard Kromberg's son?"

"It is my honor to call him Dad."

"He is a daring astrophysicist and creative inventor. And yet, I have heard rumor that his discoveries were actually influenced by *you*. Is that true?"

Reflecting little internal reaction as if he had heard the question a hundred times Bobby responded, "Rumor is misguiding, Doctor. I am merely one of his many inspirations. He is, without question, a master of his crafts."

"Humbly said, Bobby," the professor gushed.

"But overly modest, Professor," Anika added with a wondering glance. "You are not easily flattered, Bobby. But I see genius in those eyes. It's a common trait around here." Then with a satisfied smile, she nodded and said, "I am honored to meet you. I take it you are pursuing physics as well?"

"That is the broad-brush stroke for now. Like the professor, I hope to expand into other disciplines. Until then, I am blessed to have his insights . . . and his friendship."

"Bobby will excel in whatever he chooses to do." The professor exclaimed. "There is a wealthy line of courtiers vying for his attention. Let's move on. Tell me now, who is this gentleman with you?"

"May I introduce the son of a friend of mine, Caleb Hutchins. His mother influenced my decision to pursue archaeology when we were undergrads; a choice I will never regret."

Bobby and Caleb shook hands. But wanting to leave social pleasantries for another time, Anika pressed on. "Professor, the reason I have brought Caleb to see you, is to have him share his discovery with you firsthand." Professor Sholom's eyebrows raised and his eyes widened. Caleb felt awkward, feeling the conversation now moving toward him.

"Caleb, this is Professor Levi Sholom, educated in physics, professor of antiquities, expert in ancient languages and my academic father when I walked these hallowed halls."

"Pleased to meet you, sir." Caleb offered a hand.

"Cheers my good man," the professor said gripping his hand. "I hope we shall leave a keen impression on you. We should dearly love to have you here at Oxford when the time arrives for your extended education. So, if you will, please excuse my zeal for this institution. I can be a boorish bother of shameless promotion. But allow me to use Bobby as an example.

"Bobby is young for a PhD candidate. He has worked very hard and has a most profound gift handed down by his father." The professor chuckled and added, "I have more than once referred to his talents as the family's well-guarded assets . . . Well, I do believe the two of you should be splendid friends while you're here. We are very interested in your discovery and I'm sure you will find, as I do, that Bobby's input will be remarkably stimulating. That is why I have included him.

"And by the bye, Anika, we have kept your visit very hush-hush as you requested. No one knows the real reason you are here. You are simply visiting your alma mater and missing your old professor." He chuckled in self-approval of his stealth.

"Thank you, Professor. I can't overstate the importance of secrecy. And I hope you will forgive me for not sending pictures or giving you a description. I could not risk it. You know the brutal intrigues that accompany our occupation."

"Hmm, yes. Indeed I do, Doctor. It is very competitive and beguiling at times." He leaned forward and flattened both hands on his desk and stated seriously, "We know the rules of the game here, I assure you. Your project and purpose, whatever it may be, shall be safe and secure."

"Well then, Professor," Anika said, "shall we proceed?"

"Yes, of course" the Professor responded, "Let's have some tea and get started. Please be seated and I'll have my assistant get on with it." Professor Sholom stepped to the door and poked his head through. He motioned his assistant to bring tea by tipping an imaginary cup to his lips and adding, "If you would be so kind, Danny." Danny nodded in response. The professor thanked him and returned to his chair.

"Caleb, this is your bailiwick. So, when you are ready, please tell us everything. Then we will talk about how we can be of help."

Returning to his desk, the Professor said, "I'm sorry, tea is acceptable isn't it? Would any of you prefer coffee?"

Caleb asked for water while the others dismissed the alternative.

"Very good. Caleb, please . . . do go ahead."

Caleb lifted his briefcase to the professor's desk. Nervous fingers worked awkwardly at the combination.

"Take your time, Caleb," Bobby stated calmly. "Inside the brilliant minds in this room are odd yet ordinary people. Start with a short version. And as details are needed, we can ask questions."

Anika smiled and nodded while the professor said, "Good show, Bobby. Keep it simple, Caleb."

Caleb appreciated the drop in tension, took a breath then continued.

"Well, the short version is that my dad and I were out bow hunting for deer. We were having coffee at the campfire before the sun came up and a meteor lit up the sky as bright as daylight for a few seconds. After it went dark again, I guess we heard a sonic boom."

"Did you feel any atmospheric change around you?" Bobby asked.

"Yes, we did. It felt like a breeze through the trees; only different."

"Okay, go ahead."

"After a while, stuff was raining down around us and started hitting closer. Tree limbs broke and we heard large objects hitting the ground. And they started coming closer. We were standing at the time and I was too scared to move. So, Dad shoved me down and covered me with his body.

"He was hit protecting me and got knocked out. So, after I got out from under him, I checked him over. He had a serious head injury. So, I yelled for help thinking there might be other hunters around. Well, I got a response, and this guy in camo walked up and started asking me questions. And then he helped me. He prayed with me for my dad and told me things would be okay."

"What can you tell me about this hunter? What did he look like?" Bobby asked then leaned in for the answer.

"Like I said, he was wearing camo, and had a bow; it was archery season. So, I assumed his camp was nearby. He was younger than my dad and knew a lot about plants and stuff. He said he could make a poultice. He had dark hair and about average build . . . I don't remember much that could be helpful.

"You can say what you want about this," Caleb fidgeted. "But after he was done helping us, he disappeared. We never found signs of another camp in the area."

"You mean," Professor Sholom questioned, "he simply vanished into the darkness without saying goodbye?"

"No, Professor Sholom. We had decent light by then. He said goodbye and walked away. But when I ran after him to get his name, he was gone. There's no way that I could *not* have found him. I think he was an angel sent to help us find what's in this brief case."

Anika spoke up. "History is filled with the supernatural, gentlemen. I find pictures of it in archaeological digs all the time. Historically, we call them myths or legends. But archaeologically speaking, there's room for these paranormal events in the formations of civilizations. Why not events like this?

"But Caleb," Anika continued, "why don't we come back to the story later, if it's needed, and get to the discovery you found."

"The hunter and I actually found it together." Caleb opened the brief case and took out pictures to pass around. "This is what it looked like when it was in the rock."

Bobby and the professor each took a picture, surprise lighting their faces. They exchanged glances.

"When me and the hunter went into the forest to search for ingredients for the poultice that healed my dad, there were meteorite rocks everywhere. The shine of the cylinder caught my eye, so I went to see what it was. Those pictures are before we removed the rock. When the hunter picked up the rock to carry it into camp, it was still hot."

"And here are pictures of it after the rock was removed." Caleb handed out more pictures and waited for questions.

"Most unusual," the professor said. "Profoundly unique . . . I have never seen or heard of anything like it. Did you bring us a sample of the rock?"

"I brought a small bag. But airport security took it."

"Not surprising," Bobby stated.

"I'll have to send you some when I get back home."

"Thank you, Caleb," Professor Sholom said. "There is much knowledge to gain from simple rocks from outer space that were used for a shroud around a mysterious cylinder . . . Please forgive a little skepticism, Caleb, it is simply my British nature. Having the rocks would certainly help me put that aside.

"I take it you have the cylinder in your brief case."

Anika declared, "We no longer have the cylinder, Professor."

Chapter Eleven

Doctor Roos suffered Professor Sholom's rant with a blank expression. She heard his scolding about the unpardonable sin of losing a priceless artifact once before. Only then, it was deserved. When the professor's lecture gained the appropriate air of seriousness, Anika smiled with satisfaction.

The professor stopped and sighed. "The memory of your fondness for pushing my buttons is returning, Anika. I used to anticipate your wittiness and enjoy the fun." He chuckled and continued. "But I must say that I have allowed myself to become stuffy in your absence. This is your silly means of showing affection, is it not?"

Anika chuckled and leaned forward. "Sentimental affection would be out of place in the UK, Professor. I just wanted you to know how much I missed you." Sitting back in the chair, she smiled. "And if it helps, you do bring the best out of me."

Professor Sholom raised his eyebrows while clearing his throat. "Indeed. — Now if you will be so kind, Caleb, please continue while I regain my composure." Whereupon, he shook his head then whisked a hand and a quick good-natured smile at Anika.

Before Caleb started, Danny brought in tea, sugar and cream and handed each one a cup. He smiled politely at Anika when offering her cup. After he left, the discussion took on life. Caleb retold their experience at the house with just the essential details with Anika expanding on them.

At the end of the telling, Anika stated, "I would not expect you to accept as true such an incredible story. But I am a witness. And given my reputation, that should be substantial."

"That is true Doctor Roos," exclaimed the professor, "In all the years I have known you, I have never heard you make exaggerations. If you will pardon my skepticism, though, this story is either fantastic or a cruel sham. And I have seen more than my share of adventurers producing the latter."

Anika nodded and said, "There's not much room in between, is there? I agree that it is extraordinary on every level." She then concluded, "But, the proof you need is in Caleb's brief case. We brought the most important part of what was left on the table."

Caleb removed the sponge block surrounding the scroll from his briefcase. Bobby stood and slipped the case from under it while Caleb gently set it in front of the Professor. Caleb sighed to calm himself, removed the top half and stepped back.

Professor Sholom stood. Slowly bending without touching, his trained eyes and emotions objectively searching from one end of the scroll to the other. At first his face expressed the investigative nature of his profession. Then softness slowly formed until admiration took its place. Putting both hands over his mouth, he declared, "You have simply ruined my day."

He opened a desk drawer, took out his cotton gloves and slipped them on. The scroll gently left its spongy nest like lifting a sleeping baby from a cradle. With adoring eyes and raised brows he stated just above a whisper, "Oh, this is remarkable." Then louder so all could hear, he reported, "It's like a fabric . . . very supple. And unless I am mistaken, it is made of the finest gold . . . This tree that the scroll material is rolled upon should be tested; it is most unusual. — And for all of this to survive the heat of reentry is incredible . . . Oh, this is simply torture.

"And what is that fragrance?" He inhaled as he passed the scroll under his nose. "The aroma is very slight but unmistakably frankincense." He raised the scroll toward the ceiling lights. "Ahhhh, a gift fit for kings. Oh, my heart is absolutely pounding."

Bobby intruded on the professor's excited thoughts,

"Professor, It's almost time for your lecture."

"Dear me, you are right, Bobby. I'm sorry, we do not have time to do a proper investigation straight away. And I shall struggle immensely to deliver my lecture . . . Oh Bobby, you will have to help me through this. I won't be able to focus without your help."

"Could you come back this evening for a longer time with us?" Bobby asked the others. He didn't leave time for a response. "What would be a good time Professor? . . . Say six o'clock?"

"Bobby, you will have to ask Danny," the professor said while setting the scroll in its protective sponge. Without removing his stare from the scroll, he added, "I have no recollection of what my schedule is for the evening."

Bobby opened the door and motioned for Danny to come to the door. Danny caught a glimpse of what was on the Professor's desk and involuntarily gasped.

"That was careless of me," Bobby scolded himself, then said with concern, "I'm sorry you saw that, Danny. Please, let no one know about it."

"Of course, Mister Kromberg, you can count on me. My lips are sealed. — What do you desire?"

"Is Professor Sholom's schedule open this evening?"

"No, it isn't. But I can ring up his appointment and attempt a reschedule if you like."

"That would be great, Danny. Thank you." Bobby closed the door and said, "We're good for this evening."

"If you care to leave the scroll here," the Professor said pointing out a small safe. "I assure you it would be perfectly secure."

"Thank you, Professor," Doctor Roos responded. "We'll keep it with us."

"As you wish, Anika," the professor stated as he bent forward to look at the scroll again, then looked up with stern fatherliness, "Would you like an armored lory to transport you? — Do you have any comprehension as to its value? If word leaked out, you would be in grave danger."

With Caleb and Anika heading for the door, Anika stopped to respond, "Secrecy will have to be our protection for now, Professor. And, I'm getting the idea that we have *no* idea about its value."

"Precisely my point, Anika," he said with resolve.

"I am not a foreigner to danger," Anika returned.

The professor sighed. "Do be careful . . . We'll see you this evening."

Chapter 12

Caleb waited in the guest area outside the office, his brief case between his legs and partially shoved under the chair. He was heartily playing a game on his phone. And because of the ear buds, oblivious to Professor Sholom and Bobby's return.

"Good evening Caleb," Bobby said enthusiastically.

Caleb started, removed the ear buds and looked up. "Yes, it is good."

"Ready for some excitement? We have a mystery to solve."

Before Caleb could answer, the Professor asked, "Where is Doctor Roos, Caleb? Is she all right?"

"Yes, she is. She just went to the cafeteria for coffee and tea."

"Ah, you Americans and you're obsession with coffee. Ghastly stuff, if you ask me . . . Shall we get started?" Without waiting, he turned toward his office door.

Caleb got up and followed them into the office. He set his briefcase on the desk, unlocked it and opened the lid. Professor Sholom reached in, picked up the sponge protector then went around and sat in his chair. Caleb shut the briefcase and set it on the floor.

The professor retrieved a bundle of cotton gloves from a drawer and dropped them on the desk. "If you must touch the scroll, be sure to wear these gloves, they are acid free. We don't want to risk further contamination by skin oils and such."

He spread out a dark grey flannel cloth and placed the sponge block upon it. With a pleasant sigh he removed the top half of the protector, took the scroll from the bottom and set the block aside. The golden scroll laying on the dark flannel heightened its brilliance and sent a wave of awe through the room.

He held the tree of the center of the scroll with his right hand and unrolled the fabric toward his left. He said, "Hello," then studied it . . . "It's backwards."

Laying it down, he reversed the ends of the scroll. Then holding the tree in his left hand, he unrolled it again. "It's a Semitic language of some kind; written from right to left. I recognize the characters."

He pointed to the lettering then snapped up a magnifying glass and handed it to Bobby. "Take a look. The ink is exquisitely bonded to the surface like it's glued on, except it is embedded *into* the gold. — Yet it rolls up like a saturated ink . . . most peculiar. I can't wait to find out what it is made of and if it can be analyzed with current technology."

He went to a book case, removed a pair of reference books and returned to his desk. As he sat down, he stated, "If you gentlemen will make yourselves comfortable while I take a crack at this . . ."

"I think Caleb and I will step outside so we can talk without distracting you." They sat in the guest area leaving the office door open and talked briefly about family roots in the United States. After some minutes, Bobby brought up what had been on his mind.

"I've been thinking about the man you met in the forest, Caleb."

"The hunter?" Caleb asked casually.

"Yes, I often call him that."

"You know him!" Caleb perked up and looked intently at Bobby.

"I've had visits from him since I was a toddler. He is my dearest friend. And he's been visiting members of my family for generations. He always appears dressed in camo-wear and has a bow with arrows. We call him the Hunter because he's hunting for people who will believe in him."

"Believe in him?" Caleb wondered. "So, he's more than an angel."

"His name is Yeshua. You would know him as Jesus."

"That was Jesus." Caleb was caught off guard. So, Bobby let Caleb absorb the idea. "Why me, Bobby? Why was I given this scroll?"

Bobby smiled confidently. "He doesn't always tell us every-thing, but he will tell us something when its time. — One possible answer is, that you and I needed to meet each other. The message I've been carrying for years is somehow connected with the message inside that scroll and the affect that scroll will have on your life."

Caleb turned his gaze to the open door . . . the professor's face reflected intense focus between the scroll and another book; his excitement obvious. The value of what had happened to him up to this time grew larger. But the why of it needed help. "This is way bigger than me, Bobby. I'm just a sixteen-year-old kid."

Bobby laughed. "I think I know how you . . ."

"I am so sorry, guys," Doctor Roos said as she walked up briskly. She carried a tray of cups with lids. The normal addi-tives were shoved in between. "I ran into an old classmate and we had some catching up to do. Danny rescued me and I had him buy the drinks for us."

She glanced through the open door, "He looks *really* focused. Do you suppose we could intrude?"

"I know he wouldn't refuse a cup of tea," Bobby stated. The three went into the office, closed the door and sat down. They held their drinks and waited.

Professor Sholom leaned back in his chair, took a sip from his tea and said, "You haven't forgotten, my dear. Well done. Just the way I like it." He took two more sips and gazed from face to face while he watched anticipation rise. At just the right moment, he smiled a fatherly smile and said, "I am being very cruel. But I love the theatrics of a good mystery like any Englishman would.

"But what I have apprehended of this scroll so far is . . . it appears we have the gospel of Matthew in a Semitic language called Aramaic. It isn't the temple Hebrew, but the common language of its day. It's a document mentioned in the writings of the church fathers; Papius, Origen and the like. — The original version actually written by Matthew disappeared from the historical record two thousand years ago. It was thought to be burned in a purge of Jewish writings by Roman authorities.

"But given all things involved with the discovery of this scroll, we now have an uncommon opportunity. We can validate the earliest manuscripts or offer potential changes to them. A scroll of this character and magnitude, is on as keen a level as finding the Ark of the Covenant."

"Oh my," Anika gasped. "This is beyond my wildest expectations."

"Well Caleb," Bobby stated. "it seems you not only have a message from space, but a message from heaven itself. I'd like to hear Jesus' explanation of this."

"I don't know what to say," Caleb responded. "You make it sound exciting, but it feels boring. It's not exactly the action movie it's been up to now."

"You're right, Caleb," Bobby chuckled. "It seems a little anti-climactic after all you've been through."

"I disagree passionately," Professor Sholom exclaimed. "This is an incredibly significant moment!"

"I think we should celebrate," Anika exclaimed. "May I offer a toast?" She raised her coffee and removed the lid. "May the adventure begin in earnest. — Cheers."

They all replied with the same affirmation and sipped the hot brew.

"I think some cream would help this to cool down," Bobby stated.

Chapter Thirteen

Caleb was inside a trash bag. Hands were outside ruffling the black plastic. Crunchy leaves were around his ears and dots of light crossed his sight. Someone called his name; it was echoing. He was back in the forest, smelling mustiness. Other names were called, but he couldn't see faces with the names.

"Caleb!" There it was again, louder than the last time. He tried moving. He was stuck to what he was laying on. The ground shook and lights rolled back and forth above him.

A man's face appeared over him shaking his shoulder. He looked fuzzy, oddly shaped and unsteady. Somebody stood behind the man peering down, rubbing his temple with one hand and fanning himself with a piece of paper in the other.

The face became clear. It was Bobby; he looked worried. Bobby pulled on his arm and sat him upright. His head swam. *How did I get on the floor?* he thought he said out loud, but heard nothing. He looked around and spotted a woman's body a few feet away. He remembered Doctor Roos.

"Is she dead?" This time he heard his voice. It sounded weak.

"She's not responding," Bobby said.

"What happened?" Caleb wondered out loud.

"We've been gassed," Bobby announced.

Caleb struggled to get off the floor. Once up, he wobbled and flopped in a chair. "I don't understand."

The professor stumbled back to his seat and stared blankly at the desk top where something was supposed to be . . . but wasn't. His face drained of color and his expression fell as understanding struck forcefully. "The scroll is gone!"

Caleb stood, head spinning, trying to grasp what the Professor said and slowly replaying the moment. A minute ago, the scroll was on the desk and everybody was talking and drinking coffee. Now the scroll is gone and we're all having trouble thinking straight. "The coffee was drugged." he stated groggily.

"How much time has gone by?" Bobby asked.

The professor looked at the wall clock and screwed up his face. "We started at six o'clock. Anika returned after seven. It is now after nine o'clock. Maybe an hour and a half . . . Oh my, whoever took it has had a dreadful head start. And my head is far too foggy to parse through a conundrum like this."

"What does that mean?" Caleb asked.

Bobby chuckled. "It means, 'figure out a puzzling problem.' Welcome to the language of higher education, Caleb. — Maybe talking this through will help us get our minds moving again."

"There's tea in the outer office," Professor Sholom stated. "Bobby, be a good chap and make some."

"Sure Professor. Let's get up and move around. It can't hurt to get our blood circulating."

Tea was made. Caffeine would make reasoning clearer. But Doctor Roos did not stir.

"Shall we see if we can get Anika on her feet?" the professor queried.

"She obviously had a different reaction than us," Bobby commented, then looked at her with fresh concern and panicked. "Maybe she had an allergic reaction. Shouldn't we call a physician?"

"You are right Bobby," the professor exclaimed. "Her life could be in danger."

As Bobby picked up the phone, Caleb stated, "Shouldn't we call the police?"

"Let's start there," the professor ordered. "It will take care of everything."

Chapter Fourteen

A medic was giving attention to the now conscious Anika. Bobby stood nearby, listening to the medic's instructions regarding her. She would be alright, but needed watching for a while. The good news was that her delayed recovery was not due to an allergic reaction; just different than the others.

On the other side of the outer office a conversation got louder.

"Well, I have *all* the information I need to file my report," Detective Inspector Lestrade declared; obviously irritated. "Quite honestly, Professor Sholom, I don't have the man power to pursue these fairy-tale documents that have supposedly fallen from American skies.

"Priceless or not, sir, there are more serious, life and death matters to attend to. And this concern will most likely fall through the cracks, at best, if left to Scotland Yard's finest and most capable . . . And most *busy*, I might add."

Lestrade pulled out his business card and wrote on the back. "But if you are earnest about retrieving this so-called antiquity," Lestrade declared arrogantly, "call the gentleman at this number. If he finds your story interesting, he will be delighted to lend you a hand.

"And with that, sirs, I bid you good night. — Cheers."

With his closing remarks, DI Lestrade turned and walked briskly down the hall, gathering the two remaining bobbies along the way.

"Cheers," Caleb stated with loud and sarcastic annoyance.

And when Lestrade was out the door he remembered to add, "Sir."

Professor Sholom glanced at the card then looked up while laughing at Caleb's disrespectful wit. "That takes the biscuit, doesn't it? I obviously forgot the anti-colonial bigotry of Scotland Yard's finest, Caleb. I'm afraid, I should have anticipated it. But I was too fuzzy-headed to think about it. I do apologize."

"I'm really ticked off, Professor. Mostly ticked off at myself for letting this happen. I'm in this situation way over my head with nowhere to turn. It would have been safer to stay home and keep all this to myself."

The professor looked at the card again. "Ah, this might change things for you." He handed the card to Caleb. "Here's a fine chap whom I believe can be of help. He's a detective of sorts."

Caleb read it then responded, "Who is he? I don't recognize the name. Do we make an appointment?"

"There is nothing to lose. We'll call in the morning."

Anika walked up, put her hand on Caleb's shoulder and read the card. Her eyes widened. "Now there is a name of renown. Is he going to be involved?"

"I don't know as yet, Anika," the professor stated. "We'll find out tomorrow."

Anika yawned, stretched one arm and shook Caleb's shoulder with the other. "If you don't mind, Professor, would you or Bobby drop Caleb by his hotel room for me? I am exhausted."

"Yes, of course, Anika. Unless you would rather leave now, Caleb . . ."

"I'd like to stay and talk if that's alright."

"Indeed it is. — Good night Anika. Pleasant dreams."

Chapter Fifteen

Caleb stood over the professor's desk and gathered the sponge casing along with his pictures. He put it all in the briefcase and shut the lid with finality. "At least I have a new briefcase," he stated glumly. "I can use it to store what's left of the cylinder." He silently stewed for a moment. "Maybe I'll just leave it here, I don't need the reminder."

"I can't relate to what you're feeling Caleb," Bobby said as he put a hand on his shoulder. "I've never had anything so valuable stolen from me."

Caleb stared at the briefcase and responded, "I'm not sure this is about the value, Bobby. I can't wrap my head around what it's worth. A hundred dollars? A hundred million dollars? It just doesn't register. Maybe it's because the scroll is so small compared to what it might be worth. Maybe it's something else."

Caleb closed his eyes and ran the fingers of both hands through his hair, his expression questioning. "What I see is the face of the Hunter. I see Jesus's face. He found me and gave me something important. And I lost it to thieves who were smarter than me." He shook his head with a lopsided smile. "That isn't saying much. I'm just a kid. And I just don't get it."

"Mary was just a kid," Bobby intruded, "when she was given the Son of God. Her and Joseph had to have some misgivings when their first years were in hiding to prevent something from happening to him. And she wasn't much older than you when their journey began. Imagine how she felt, though, when Jesus died on a cross before her very eyes; how inadequate she felt to prevent it from happening. And how she must have grieved to lose him without hope of recovery."

Caleb took a breath, lifted his head and looked Bobby in the eye. "I think I do. She lost everything she lived for. Death stole it all away."

"Sure, she had other children," Bobby continued. "But when she lost her promised object of motherhood, her heart was devastated. She carried more than thirty years of promises from God about him. Their fulfillment was now in question. That's a loss only Mary could grasp. Yet, what she couldn't see was that it was just the beginning for all the children of God that Jesus would give birth to from then on. But she didn't know that at the time. She would see a bigger picture later on. And there's always a bigger picture. — Could this be a good time to look for it?"

"I wouldn't know where to begin," Caleb responded.

"If you strip away the gold, what's left?"

Caleb opened his hands, bobbled his head and looked quizzical. "If it was just a book and not a golden scroll? It would be Matthew in Aramaic. The Word of God."

"Good point. According to John, the Word *is* God. It is a picture of Jesus. It's the life in Jesus given to us. It is a window into the heart of God. It's a revelation of his love for us. It is a treasure of deeper value than can be understood."

Caleb's eyes said he was getting at least some of what Bobby said. "Okay, that's a bigger picture. How big does it get?"

"No matter how big it appears to get, Caleb, it's always bigger. For a treasure seeker who mines for gold in truth and Spirit, the riches of the Kingdom are inexhaustible. Sometimes you find nuggets and sometimes you find veins. King David says, 'Your promises are the source of my bubbling joy; the revelation of your word thrills me like one who has discovered hidden treasure.'[1]"

"How do you discover hidden treasure, Bobby?"

"Tenacity, wisdom and good tools. — God conceals the revelation of his word in the hiding places of his glory. But the honor of kings is revealed by how they thoroughly search out the deeper meaning of all that God says."[2]

"Papa God loves to conceal things for those who truly want to search for them. It's not the golden scroll that is valuable; it's the true wealth inside."

"Bobby, you said something about mining for gold in truth and Spirit. Finding what's in the golden scroll is about searching for the deeper meanings of his word and finding the hiding places of his glory if I'm hearing you right."

"Yes, and so much more."

"I get that he hides things for us to discover. That's really cool. But, I'm not getting something. I don't understand what 'hiding places of his glory' means."

"Okay," Bobby said thoughtfully. "In the Hebrew, honor and glory are the same word. Honor is defined as high respect, esteem and the understanding of great privilege.

"Kings understand privilege. They understand when honor is extended; both in the giving and receiving of it. Kings understand the wisdom of searching and the heart of a seeker. They understand the satisfaction of possessing something that was difficult and costly to come by. Kings value a gift with meaning that is deeper than its appearance and unpacking its significance."

Caleb put his hands in his pockets, looked down but saw nothing; just finding a spot to focus on. "Then, if we are miners of the golden scroll, digging for the deeper meanings of all that God says, and because he is making that available if we will want it and value it, we are honoring him and he is honoring us."

Bobby's head nodded in approval.

"Does that make us kings?" Caleb asked.

"Royalty Caleb. Royal sons and daughters."

"Royal miners," Caleb injected, "with special privileges.

"And special conditions, Caleb. Since we are his true children, we qualify to share *all* his treasures. For indeed, we are heirs of God himself. And since we are joined to Christ, we also inherit all that he is and all that he has. We will experience being co-honored with him provided that we accept his sufferings as our own."[3]

"Suffering? Wait a minute."

"Think about it. If we truly want to know what Jesus values, what *we* value will suffer. God's truth is alive. It gets in between our earthly nature and heavenly nature — then shows us the choices. In those choices we can possess what Jesus values; life or death. At the risk of over-simplifying, working through those choices will cause suffering."

Caleb looked stumped. He met Bobby's eye, then looked away shaking his head. "How did I get signed up for this?"

Bobby laughed.

Chapter Sixteen[1]

Author's note: This part of the story was a documented case with Sherlock Holmes. Doctor Watson sent Caleb a copy for advanced approval. Although never published, Caleb thought the doctor captured what happened next accurately and remembered this encounter with great fondness. So, the story continues in Watson's unique fashion.

* * * * * * * * *

The morning started casually for myself and distinguished friend at the rooms of number 221B Baker Street. While I had chosen to sleep in, Mister Sherlock Holmes had been up and eaten his breakfast. Mine was covered at the table — and likely cold. Although my friend is brilliant in the arts of observation, he comes by it through singular focus and an oft-distraction from personal considerations.

As I dined, he sat in his armchair, legs drawn up and absorbed in the morning newspaper. His side leaned to the right, toward the broad windows of our sitting room for best reading light. In his conventional behavior, he would alternate glances between the newspaper and the windows while regarding new information.

"Watson," Holmes said, breaking his concentration. "It seems I have an appointment with a certain professor this morning.

"Not that Moriarty fellow?" I responded anxiously.

"Heavens no, my good Doctor. This is an Oxford chap with an expertise in antiquities, a Professor Levi Sholom. And he will be attended with a company of three Americans."

"When is your appointment scheduled?"

"That should be them ringing at the door. Mrs. Hudson will show them up."

"I shall take a tray for my breakfast and retire to my room." I said, wishing to not intrude.

"I'll hear nothing of it, Watson. Your presence would be of great benefit to me. According to Lestrade's report, their story will prove to be a profound fantasy or a most uncommon super-natural phenomenon. You will assist me in determining which."

With her familiar rap at the door, Mrs. Hudson lead the way with three gentlemen at the tow. They entered and she departed with a request from Holmes that she bring them tea.

A distinguished looking man with grizzled hair and profound nose entered first. He was thin, lively of step and a bit fidgety. Compared to the other two he would be the obvious choice for a professor. Another appeared to be in his mid twenties and of slight build. His countenance was remarkably peaceful and confident for his years. The third was a youth of his late teens, ruddy complected, muscular and very anxious.

"Professor Sholom, I presume," Holmes said with hand extended.

"Indeed, Mister Holmes. What a remarkable pleasure to make your acquaintance. I would never have dreamed of meeting you face-to-face."

The professor made introductions all around and we seated ourselves at the end of its momentum.

"I was of the persuasion there was to be a fourth person, Professor," said Holmes.

"Ah, yes, Mister Holmes. Doctor Anika Roos should have

come as well."

"She's an archaeologist?" Holmes asked.

"She is indeed. You know about her, then?"

"We have a mutual acquaintance . . . She could not come, I take it."

"It's like this, you see. We were all drugged last night. And apparently her reaction to whatever it was we were given has left her — somewhat challenged. But I do believe between the three of us, we can communicate all there is to know of this dreadful business."

"Indeed . . . Mister Lestrade sent me the details in his report. I regret that his bias regarding the incident has defiled the data. So, if you will, let us hear a clear account of what has befallen you. Spare no detail, no matter how trivial you may think it to be."

Starting with the arrival of the cylinder, each person gave an account of what they knew and experienced. Mister Sherlock Holmes probed for more data with his precisely measured questions.

"Is that a sample of the coffee in question, Caleb?" he asked pointing to the sealed container in his hand.

"Yeah, I thought you might want to have it analyzed." Caleb responded.

"Good show, Caleb. Good show. We shall do that immediately," Mr. Holmes said. "Doctor, Watson, if you will."

I took the cup to the table and set it in a safe spot.

"Now gentlemen, time is of the essence. I have all the data I need and I must act swiftly. If all parties involved will be at the

Professor's office at eight o'clock this evening, I will present my findings and have a solution . . . I must insist that Doctor Roos be present regardless of how she's feeling."

"Are you saying," Professor Sholom asked in astonishment, "that you have solved the theft?"

"Indeed I have. Gentlemen, we must be on our way immediately. There is no more time to waste. Your plight has been leaked to the media dramatists and we shall be delayed by them if we do not hurry."

"How do you know . . ."

"No more questions." Sherlock rejoined. "We are seconds away from disaster. Watson, grab your hat, we must go — now."

Holmes and I flew down the stairs. "Let yourselves out as best you can," Holmes yelled back as we went. Outside the door, we hailed a taxi, bungled our way into the seat as Sherlock gave the destination.

"Briony Lodge on Serpentine Avenue. And make it sharp."

The driver hit the gas and surged forward, then suddenly jerked to a stop. A door swung open and Caleb jumped inside demanding, "I'm going with you!"

As we drove away, he turned to look back. "It's just as you said Mister Holmes. Bobby and the professor are surrounded."

Holmes pulled the gold chain attached to his pocket watch and removed it from his vest. He tapped it several times to send a text and shut the cover, "Watson, we must be in position and coordinated with Lestrade if we are to apprehend the scoundrels."

"Holmes, the address you gave is the home of Irene Adler." I said with surprise. "What on earth has she to do with this business?”

"I don't have time to explain, my dear Watson. I must make connection with Lestrade if we are to have a successful conclusion."

Upon his statement, Mister Holmes spent the remaining time talking to his pocket watch. When he snapped it shut, the young man asked, "How can I help?"

"I insist that you do absolutely nothing," Holmes declared sternly. "Just observe and learn."

Sympathetic for the boy's concern of his lost artifact and the intimidation of Holmes's rudeness I engaged the youth. "Please tell me your name again." Although I remembered his name, it was a starting point for a conversation.

"It's Caleb. — Mister Holmes, you mentioned Lestrade. Are you referring to the Inspector at Scotland Yard?"

"Undoubtedly he told you he would not help; stubbornly conventional. He's a decent enough inspector, but short-sighted in the science of deduction and analysis when it comes to the apprehension of skilled criminals. But, rest assured, he will be with us to gain the arrest and pocket the credit. In that regard, he is highly predictable.

"Aside from that, how you came into possession of this artifact was in Lestrade's report. A most unusual story. I would be intrigued to hear your version of it when we are done with this.

"If I may be direct, you are obviously naïve and don't comprehend that you are in this business beyond your capabilities. When dealing with the kind of money this scroll is worth, big money attracts big wolves." Sherlock sighed and finished, "I pray you survive without being torn to shreds — or worse, falling jaded beyond repair in the regard of your fellow man."

Holmes suddenly shifted and declared, "Stop driver, stop." We were about one hundred yards from Briony Lodge. The driver pulled over and we finished our journey on foot to insure our stealth.

"Watson, we must use topmost care and trickery from here. As you remember, this woman has been a painful nemesis. Her wit has beaten me in the past and I shall not underplay her again. — I am looking forward to her capture and her conspirators."

As we rounded the corner by the lodge, we were confronted with the unexpected scene of police vehicles outside the gates. A man and woman were being engaged with hand cuffs.

I looked at Holmes and saw immediately the muscles of his jaw tighten. He ran to the group and indignantly scolded, "Lestrade, what idiocy is this about?" With hands and arms saying as much as his anger he demanded, "Explain yourself. Why didn't you wait to arrest Miss Adler along with these?"

Lestrade spun and returned hotly, "Because I have a job to do, Mister Holmes! We have the perpetrators and this ridiculous scroll. I am quite satisfied with the collar even if you are not.

"I see this is more about Irene Adler than the arrest. She has eluded you again hasn't she. She's not the beast you make her, Holmes. You should know that she also tipped us off about these two. I say a thank you would be in order."

Sherlock quieted with a slump of his shoulders as Lestrade walked away in a huff. "She's done it again, Watson. She anticipated my move. I tell you the woman is diabolical. There's nothing more to be done. — Where is Caleb?"

Given the squad of bobbies and spectators, there was some crowd to get through to find Caleb. I spotted him and tugged Holmes' arm. "He's with Lestrade."

We converged as Inspector Lestrade and Caleb approached the thieves. Caleb carried a bag I presumed held the scroll. He stopped short. His face showed utter shock.

"Anika!"

Chapter Seventeen

After all was finished at Briony Lodge, we hailed a taxi and climbed aboard. "We dare not go back to Baker Street," Sherlock declared. "Let's spare engaging the advancing hordes of media, Watson. Doctor Roos most certainly told them where to find you, Caleb. Had I not deduced the scheme in the nick of it, we shall have missed our escape. Instead, we will proceed to Oxford. However, I fear these chaps may be thorns in our feet for the remainder of your stay in England."

To soften the coarseness of Sherlock's debriefing I offered something practical. "I will call ahead and arrange for security to be waiting for us, Sherlock. But may I suggest that the thing weighing heavy on Caleb's mind is this recent betrayal?"

"Ah yes, Watson. Thank you for reminding me . . . My condolences, Caleb, and my apologies. Like a blood hound on a scent, I am often out of touch with those around me. How are you doing?"

"I've never experienced anything like it," Caleb responded gruffly. "I'm mad . . . How could she be so nice and screw me so bad? . . . I trusted her . . . My family trusted her . . . My mother . . . If she hears about this through the media before I get a chance to talk to her, things won't go well for me."

I reached out hoping to console the young man. Young or old, wounds of betrayal are not easily resolved. "Caleb, take care to not make this a disaster. I'm sure it will turn out to be a mole hill and not the mountain you now see. The scroll has been returned. You can move forward again."

"Doctor Watson," Caleb responded reeling back his emotions. "It's like Mister Holmes said, 'big money attracts big wolves.' I now have a firm picture in my mind of an ugly wolf that looked like a pretty sheep." He bucked up at this point and continued admirably. "But you know what? . . . I'm determined to see this through. 'It ain't over until it's over.' My dad has always taught me that. Sheep, wolves or thieves, I'm not quitting; I'm not giving in. I'm not going home until this game is played to the end."

I have rarely seen an eye of respect in Mister Sherlock Holmes. He does not give that honor easily. I saw a mere hint of it today. Turning back to Caleb I said, "Well said my good man. Rest assured, we shall stand with you also; whenever and wherever it is needed."

"Now Caleb," Sherlock spoke suddenly, "I would be fascinated to hear the story of how you came by this scroll. Spare no detail, no matter how trivial you may think it to be. I must hear the whole of it."

Caleb proceeded to fascinate, indeed. His story was clearly difficult to accept at face value, but so profound he could not have fabricated it. Mister Holmes conveyed the depth of his thoughts through silence. I dare say he was quiet for the remainder of our trip to Oxford.

Chapter Eighteen

The trio was met by a quartet of campus security and police to escort them to Professor Sholom's office. "I am Sergeant Moynihan. We are instructed to remain with you," she stated firmly after opening the cab door, "until the item you brought is secure to our satisfaction. At the request of the college, please do not answer the media's questions. An official address of the issue will be given later."

"As you wish," Doctor Watson responded.

A crowd pressed them from the cab to the building entrance. As reporters buzzed with rapid-fire questions, video cams recorded silent and serious faces in return. Extra officers waited at the door to let them in. Their four-minute arrival was annoying, yet uneventful.

Sergeant Moynihan followed Caleb into the professor's office while the others waited.

"Professor Sholom," Caleb said with a sigh of relief and a twisted smile as he put the bag on his desk. "This needs to go in your safe."

The professor put on his cotton gloves, transferred the scroll to the safe and locked it. He nodded to the sergeant, who took the cue and stepped outside then asked, "Do you want me to wait for you, Mister Holmes?"

"Indeed," he responded. "Give me just a few moments." With a nod to Doctor Watson, he stepped into the professor's office. Watson followed and shut the door.

"Mr. Holmes," Professor Sholom began. "We are dearly grateful for your mastery in repossessing this treasure. I have questions but don't know where to begin. Please help us understand what has transpired."

"Gentlemen, I'll make my report brief and we will be on our way. Doctor Anika Roos and Mister Danny Rance are in the custody of Scotland Yard facing charges of larceny, conspiracy and grand theft. You will likely not see them again for some time."

"The look of shock on your faces is expected. Your mention of her name at my flat brought to mind an incident some years ago that never came to public light.

"The South American incident of the lost artifact?" Professor Sholom inquired. "I was unaware you were involved."

"Precisely the incident. And yes, I was involved."

"I was told it was taken by thieves in a moment of careless security."

"Anika's involvement could not be proven. Local authorities, whom I believe were bought off, insisted the case be closed and that was the end of it. I was asked to intervene, but could not get away. So, the artifact in question was never recovered. My personal investigation later on stopped at the door of Irene Adler; the exact location where the arrests were made this time.

"Had she and Danny completed their transaction, the scroll would have disappeared in a bottomless pit of black market transactions."

"Oh, there must be more detail than that, Mister Holmes."

"Professor, let us be content with the return of the scroll and the apprehension of two of the three conspirators. To say more would reveal my disappointment of an imperfect outcome and an inept constabulary. Perhaps another time.

"Caleb can fill you in about the matter. — And with that my dear sirs, Doctor Watson and I will be on our way. The concern on your faces when we walked in indicate you have other things pressing. So, we shall leave you to it."

"Mister Holmes," Professor Sholom extended his hand, "and Doctor Watson, it has been an honor. You are as extraordinary as your reputation declares. Thank you again."

As the door closed, Professor Sholom stated, "Caleb, my good man. You have weathered a severe storm and made it home to celebrate. Please be seated and listen carefully. — We now have another storm to face."

Chapter Nineteen

The professor sat down, leaned back, put his elbows on the arms of the chair and touched his fingers together. His face mirrored a depth in the *what next?* concern he had to talk about. "Our encounter with the media this morning had an unexpected twist in it. The questions about your scroll were answered as best we could without your input. But a peculiar question was put to us about the relationship your event had to the breaking news that came from the colonies last night. It was an announcement given by Bobby's father about an event that happened some years ago."

Caleb perked up and looked at Bobby; eager to learn more.

The professor lifted a hand in Bobby's direction and stated, "Bobby and I have discussed it at length. But if you will Bobby, explain it again for Caleb."

Bobby calmly responded, "Dad released a statement last night in the States about a cosmic event he and I witnessed several years ago. I was too wrapped up with our own problems yesterday to check the message that would have forewarned me. So, it came as a surprise to get it first-hand from the media.

"But going back to when he and I had that experience, my dad thought it best to put off announcing the implications of that event until solid scientific information could be communicated and reasonable solutions presented. Experts, that my father trusted, were too few and ill-equipped to move anything forward in a reasonably safe way at the time.

"Because my name was released in association with the theft of your scroll and the unusual circumstances of how you came by it, curiosity worked up the astrophysics community."

"I'm sure jealousy and revenge was a factor," Professor Sholom added.

"I hope they are better people than that, professor," Bobby responded. "But it may have had some influence.

"You see, Caleb, my dad upset some people to get time in the observatory we used. And the fact that we kept our findings secret could have kept the grudge factor alive.

"The story of the scroll and my participation reactivated memories. A committee voted to over-ride the protection of the files we created that night. And when the videos were brought to light, Dad was forced to give an account."

"So, what's the big deal?" Caleb rejoined. "There was little attention given to the meteorite that brought my scroll until Lestrade leaked the theft. *Are* they related?"

"Not really. The shower that brought your scroll is fairly common; asteroids pass by earth all the time. Some go undetected until the last minute. Smaller chunks, like yours, get into the atmosphere and give us something to look at. But real cosmic threats are rare and fewer still actually hit our planet."

"Threats?" Caleb interjected. "What kind of threats?"

"The event my dad and I saw have direct effects on the future health and well-being of every person of this planet."

"How do you know?" Caleb challenged.

"My story has similarities to yours, Caleb. The Hunter appeared to me when I was twelve and gave me a note with the terrestrial coordinates, date and time to be looking at the sky. What we witnessed happened just as the note said.

"Jesus told me at the time it would change the way we live."

"When will this happen?" Caleb asked.

"My father was tracking it when he could. Currently, the sun is between us and that rock. And when that changes in a couple of months, verification and analysis will flood in from all over the world."

"I'm not following how that is connected to me."

"Nor I," added the professor.

"It's the idea of it, mostly," Bobby responded. "However remote, the prospect of a global cataclysm stirs up emotions and demands a response. Whether it's your event or mine is not important. The tribes of the earth want answers and solutions. And the media of the earth want stories. Put that together and you have breaking news."

"And the Word of God," the professor interjected, "has the answers."

"Precisely. Attention will be drawn to Spirit and truth. The Word will have answers in regard to how the world faces the crisis; the Spirit has solutions about how to repair the damage when it comes; or prevent it if that should be the case."

"But the golden scroll is only the book of Matthew," Caleb exclaimed. "I'm missing something."

"The scroll is a prophetic picture of your message to the people, Caleb. It's so subtle and yet so profound, it cannot be dismissed. We have been given a great treasure through supernatural means. The golden scroll is a reminder of who has the answer; the Spirit; and what is the solution; the revelation of truth. Professor Sholom has wisdom for unlocking the gold from that gift and how to share it with others."

"Okay," Caleb mused to himself, "Bobby shows me how the Spirit works, and the professor teaches me how the Word works."

"Indeed, Caleb." The Professor commented. "I have spent years preparing others for these times. What a wonderful sense of privilege that thought gives me. And what about you Bobby? What is your role in these difficult days?"

"I'm a solutionary. This isn't doomsday, Professor. This is a rude awakening that will be followed by a reformation. Those who trust in Jesus won't be hurt by this event; and when the people of this planet turn to God, they won't be hurt either. That is my message. But I have a practical work to do as well. When this is over, the world will require substantial repair. We will all have a lot of work to do in a season of restoration for this planet."

"Hold on!" Caleb exclaimed. "I'm having a hard time getting this information to land. I'm just the kid with the scroll. I'm not a scientist or a professor. You're making me bigger than I really am."

"You're a world changer, Caleb," Bobby resounded with a hand lifted toward him. "You don't need a PhD or special qualifications. Just say yes to God, follow him and you'll help lead the way; we all will."

"Stop, stop, stop!" Caleb pleaded with his hands raised. "You're moving way too fast. I didn't come here for this."

"Caleb," Professor Sholom reacted, "with all that is in motion and all that is yet ahead, this is not a time to stop — nor even a time to hesitate. It is time to act."

Caleb got up and reached for the door. "I need a minute. My heads spinning." He went into the outer office and stood at the windows. It was evening. The sun had set, yet still light outside. Seeing trees and grass and sky relieved the tension in his shoulders, but his thoughts raced.

He thought about the intensity of his life since the cylinder landed and what he's been through. He never knew betrayal like Anika handed him. Trust took a nasty fall. Thanks to Sherlock Holmes and Doctor Watson, he's the other side. Losing the scroll put him through a whirlwind of loss and failure and feeling stupid. Recovering it renewed his resolve to be more alert and keep going. Yet, he had to grasp that what lay ahead might be tougher still; most likely would be.

The concern on his mother's face wasn't hard to see; he had seen it many times. If she had heard about the theft, she already knew about Anika. She would blame herself and react to protect him from further problems. Safe and secure was what she would want for him. Agreement with that idea would be tempting and life so much easier.

If I accept what Bobby and the professor are saying, there would be a new reality. The peace and quiet of family life would never be the same. School would definitely never be the same. What would people think of me? I'm part of some nut-case conspiracy? I could walk away and go home; distance myself from this place and these people. In the process I would save face with little explanation and be comfortable; another tempting thought.

He remembered what he said to Doctor Watson in the taxi on the way back to Oxford: *I'm not quitting. I'm not giving in. I'm not going home until this game is played to the end.*

Doctor Watson's pledge to stick it out with him reminded him that he wasn't alone. Given their integrity, that pledge was probably rock solid. He remembered the point his dad made when they were hunting and he was fighting the distraction to break rock off the scroll: "We're here to help each other." He saw the face of the Hunter, and remembered the healing of his dad. *Jesus, you're in all this. I'm not alone. Where is all this going? Everything looks like a train wreck with a debris field.*

And now . . . there's a planet to save. "Come on," he growled at the world beyond the window. "I'm just a blade of grass in a huge meadow."

He sighed with resolve and turned back to the Professor's office, sat down and stated, "I need to talk with my mom and dad."

Professor Sholom smiled, "That's a splendid idea. Let's go by your hotel room, pick up your stuff and check out. You can stay at my home and do a video connection from there. It is time to bring your family into this."

Chapter Twenty

The journey to Professor Sholom's estate gave Bobby a window to fill in some gaps of his cosmic adventure. While the professor drove, Bobby told of the night he received his note from the Hunter. Then laid open the fallout he had with his father after their trip, and what he had to work through at the time. The professor had heard parts of the story before, yet attentively listened.

Caleb pondered Bobby's story carefully while his eyes glanced between Bobby and the rustic surroundings of the English countryside. By the time they saw the gate to the house, pieces of what Bobby said developed a corelating picture in Caleb's mind. There were similarities, but the picture wasn't large enough to help grasp what questions he needed to ask.

Caleb sighed as the professor keyed the remote for the gate. Lingering reporters bellowed questions at him through the closed windows in hopes of creating a story. In Caleb's mind the story wasn't finished; it would be pointless to answer them.

The gate closed as they drove the fifty yards to the front door. Persistent questions hammered from the safe zone between them and the world outside. The drone of human noise disagreed with the haven of the countryside.

Gina was the quiet strength of the Sholom marriage and missed little in personal considerations of her friends, acquaintances and strangers. With stately beauty and dignity, she made hospitality look easy and put her guests at ease. People visiting her home always wanted to return.

When the men arrived, Gina Sholom had afternoon tea waiting. Afterward, she showed Caleb his room and the conveniences while probing graciously to see how he was holding up. The explanation of responsibilities and liberties for young guests, as she had done dozens of times over the years, was given with warmth and respect. The pleasant dialogue added assurance that she not spend needless time picking up after her guests. Confident that Caleb was comfortably at home and versed on how to take care of his hosts, she gave him a hug and departed for a previously scheduled engagement.

With belongings deposited on the bed, he shut the door and went to find Bobby. He found him in the study arranging chairs and cameras for the link-up with Caleb's parents. Professor Sholom was also there and occupied at his desk with a keyboard. Caleb grabbed the camera controller and fidgeted with its joysticks and buttons; keeping his hands busy while he pondered what he would say. What his parents knew or didn't know was all second-guess. And the bad news that tumbled around in his mind outweighed the good.

"It's so nerve wracking!" Caleb exclaimed with his fists raised.

"What is it, Caleb?" the professor asked.

"Not knowing how they're going to respond."

"We are ready for the link-up, Caleb," Bobby laughed. "There's no more time to think about it."

"What time is it there?" Caleb asked, wondering if his parents were losing sleep.

"It's late morning," the professor responded with patient understanding. "Caleb, I've been a parent for a long time. Trust me, your parents will do just fine."

The three sat in respective chairs, with Caleb in the middle. His mom and dad were happy to see him and greeted the others pleasantly. Caleb introduced Bobby and Professor Sholom. Incidental chatter briefly carried the conversation. And then David got to the point. "We heard about the theft of the scroll and the arrest of Anika. It's breaking news here, and having Sherlock Holmes master the recovery of it has enlarged the headlines. In spite of it, we are still shocked that Anika could do that to us."

"Caleb," Layla interjected. "What happens now? Where are you staying?"

"If I may answer the latter question, Mrs. Hutchins," the professor stated. "Caleb is a welcome guest in my home. And as you can see, it is quite comfortable. He will not be a burden. And my wife will see to it that he is looked after. She's not in, presently. But she said she would be happy to chat with you at your convenience."

"It would soothe my concerns if we could, Professor Sholom."

"I understand, Mrs. Hutchins. — Now if you will. Bobby and I will leave the three of you to have a private word. And we will be back to answer whatever questions you have."

"Thank you," David stated.

As Bobby and the professor left the study, Layla resumed the conversation. "I am so sorry for what Anika put you through. That must have . . ."

"She was flawless, Mom. *Nobody* saw through her deception. If it weren't for perfect timing and dealing with someone smarter than her, she would have gotten away with it. — And I learned some things about people I'll never forget. But I'm over this and determined to keep going.

"Professor Sholom said that with the existence of the scroll now public knowledge, there will be more media attention to deal with. It's worth will be talked about. And as Mister Holmes says, 'big money attracts big wolves.' And . . ."

"You're scaring me, Caleb," Layla interrupted. "You have no idea what *that* looks like from *here*," she added forceful hand gestures. Then she turned and demanded, "David, we need to bring our son home."

"I have the scroll, Mom." Caleb rejoined, protecting his position. "Bringing it home doesn't change anything. It's sinking in that my life will not be the same because of it. And you guys need to think about it, too. I don't know where we're going because of it, but there's no turning back."

"Yes there is, Caleb," David declared. "Leave the scroll there, cut your losses and leave. It's that simple."

"I can't leave the scroll," Caleb whined. "Besides, I can't leave until the police say I can leave because of Anika."

"Certainly," Layla exclaimed weightily, "the police can see the burden that puts on us. I want contact information of all officials involved so I can talk with them. There *must be* another way."

"Mom — Dad, I know you want me safe and protected. But, one thing I've discovered since I've been here is there's a higher level of life than that. I'm not coming home without the scroll, and I want to finish what I came here for." And with a pumped fist he added, "This ain't over until it's over."

Caleb caught the slightly upturned lips of a smile and the gleam in his dad's eye that said *my son is growing up*. He knew he had an ally.

"So, Caleb," Layla challenged, "what *did* you go there for?"

"Whatever it is, it's bigger and more valuable than a golden scroll. This is about lessons in life I can't learn anywhere else."

Layla furrowed her brow and shook her head. "These are dangerous lessons, Caleb."

"I'm in good hands and have the support of England's best and smartest."

"Caleb," David said calmly, "I am confident you can handle whatever comes at you."

"David!" Layla moaned.

David held up a hand and pressed forward. "It's stuff like this that makes men out of boys. Conflict and challenge are things a man should run to; not away from." He turned to Layla and added, "Caleb's a man and it's time to give him enough rein to steer his way through this on his own. He can *do* this."

"I *can't* do this," Layla returned hotly.

"I understand, Layla, it'll be harder on you than him. But we've been training him for this moment for a long time. He's ready, but we're not. It's the right time."

"Not going to happen," Layla protested while David turned back to Caleb.

"Caleb, you don't have to pull anything off perfectly. Just do your best with what you have and what you know. Rely on your team players and trust their advice."

Caleb cleared his throat. "Thanks for believing in me, Dad. — Mom, I can't stop you from worrying about me. I know that. Please, please understand. This is important."

"Why is it important, Caleb? Can you help me? I don't understand."

"I don't know. It just is. I can see it, but I can't explain it yet."

"So, you feel you were made for this or something," Layla concluded sarcastically.

"These circumstances were certainly made outside the ordinary boxes, Layla," David stated. "And they all point to Caleb. He *is* made for this."

"I don't care about that. I just want my son home." David and Layla looked at each other. "And I can see by the look on your face, you aren't going to change your mind."

Silence hung in the air as the course was set. David restarted the dialogue, "Caleb, this would be a good time to bring Professor Sholom and Bobby back in. I have a question or two for them."

Caleb went to the door and looked out. With no one around, he went to the kitchen.

"Thank you," David began when they were reseated, "for helping Caleb through these difficult days. It must be quite a change to your routine."

"A little difficulty has made us quite the chums, Mr. Hutchins," the professor responded.

David nodded, then Layla asked looking for reinforcement, "What about Caleb's education while he's with you?"

"Please forgive my arrogance, Mrs. Hutchins. But this is Oxford University; education comes naturally. While certain basic elements of his education may be suspended while he's here, some very advanced learning and thinking concepts will be implanted in this young man that will attend him for the rest of his days.

"But on the practical note, Caleb will help me translate the scroll, and Bobby will teach him invaluable principles in the science of deduction and analysis. In the same vein of things, he will get a fair taste of inspiration from the Oxford culture of world changers."

"Professor," Layla chimed in skeptically, "I take it you're thinking Caleb is a future world changer?"

"My dear Mrs. Hutchins. With all that has transpired and yet is to come, I dare say he has already *become* one."

"That doesn't relieve my fears in the slightest, professor."

"It was not meant to. There is nothing I can say or do that will remove the risk factor from those who are determined to meet life straight up. Change is always resisted. Only courage and a never-give-up character makes all the difference, or the world around us will be molded by other agents. One way or another, the world will change and those who do nothing will live the consequence."

The professor sighed. "I hope you can understand my directness. My point is to simply state the way things to be."

"Your point is understood, professor," Layla responded with a small level of tenderness. "It doesn't make the bitter pill any sweeter."

The professor smiled and said, "Stated like a true Brit, Mrs. Hutchins."

Layla shook her head in response.

David questioned the professor further about official documents for Caleb's school and let the conversation wind down.

After good-byes were said, it was time for tea and debriefing in front of the fireplace.

"My parents haven't heard about the asteroid," Caleb announced. "They would have mentioned it if they did."

"That's a good sign," Bobby stated. "Politics and other headlines are keeping the asteroid story hidden. We have time to prepare a strategic plan about what to do and what we're going to say. — Caleb, you'll have an opportunity to meet my dad. He's an amazing man . . . like your dad."

"Caleb," the professor queried. "you had something on your mind when we were at the office. Would you care to talk about it?"

"Professor, I wasn't getting this world changer thing. Since I've come here, this world got bigger and people more complicated. And with a cosmic event that can threaten our planet?" He shook his head, "That's just crazy! . . . I'm in over my head. I feel like running home where life is simple, small and comfortable. But I can't stop thinking that there's a big question camped in front of me waiting for my answer.

"So, before I pull the trigger on this, I thought talking with my parents would help."

"Did it?"

"If my dad had not supported me, I would be getting a flight home. And it was hard watching my mom go through this. I can see that she's scared. — But I know my parents. They'll work through it; they always do."

"And what about you?" Bobby asked with a smile. "What's your answer to the big question?"

"I'm in."

Chapter Twenty-one

Garage walls and high stone fences echoed the unique ping of basketball dribbling on the concrete. Taunts, backboard and rim thumps, the swish of spiked shots and shoe squeaks was the active noise of competition. Sweat ran in spite of the fall chill and the sun losing its grip on daylight.

It had been a week since Caleb had talked with his parents; most of that time spent at the Sholom house. Frequent guests popped in to see Mrs. Sholom. Often driven by curiosity, they really sought a glimpse of the scroll.

"It's kept in the safe at the professor's office," was a typical aversion to other annoying questions he didn't want to answer. It didn't always work. A daily diminishing group of news people hovered at the gate, stifling any walks he could have had around the area. And there were challenging moments at the Sholom house, as he strived to stay occupied until Bobby or the professor showed up.

Bobby recognized the boredom trap and discovered basketball as a common interest. Professor Sholom graciously brought in a portable hoop. "It's not an especially British wicket," he stated at the time. "But I'll spread the word and see if we could borrow a goal; if that's what you call it."

The hoop showed up, and the games began.

Another swoosh of the net and Caleb called out, "Yeah, game and series! Two games to one."

"Way to go, Caleb," Bobby responded breathing hard. "When I shed my stuffy physics cap, basketball is actually a lot of fun."

"What do you mean, Bobby? I though you played a lot."

"I play basketball to think about other things. I's pretty casual, really; no hurry, no game plan, just occupied while I process my thoughts. But playing with you is another thing. Winning wasn't on my mind . . . until the second game. That's when I focused up. It's amazing what you can do when you block out everything else."

"You're saying that you decide to be competitive and kick it in like turning on a light switch?" was Caleb's response. "Come on."

"Something like that. Concentration takes practice. Once you get it, you can do it anywhere for anything. And I have a lot of practice at concentration."

"I practice a *lot* to get better at this game. Anticipation and reaction is what this game is about. And doing the basics over and over again."

"If I can picture it, I can do it," Bobby said with a shrug of disagreement. "It's a gift."

"That's lame. You worked me *hard* for game three. — Anyway, thanks for making it real."

Bobby extended his fist and the two did high and low knuckle bumps. "Let's do it again tomorrow."

"Is it always this cold?"

"Just wait until the fog shows up," Bobby responded. "That will be something to text home about."

As they started through the kitchen, Bobby asked, "You want something hot to drink?"

"That sounds good. How about some hot chocolate?"

Bobby smiled remembering, "That sounds like something my grandma would ask. — I sure miss her cookies."

"I don't see my grandparents much," Caleb stated matter-of-factly. "They live near the rest of the family. Great people though. It must have been nice to have your grandma in the same neighborhood."

"She was always there for me when I needed someone to talk to. She'd listen for a while, then say, 'This is a two-cookie conversation,' sometimes three cookies, and pull out the chocolate to go with them. — You're going to meet her someday. You'll like her."

Caleb settled in at the bay windows of the breakfast nook while Bobby started the chocolate. Looking into the professor's back yard, Caleb confessed, "I've never been away from home and on my own like this before. It's really cool." He thought a moment, then smiled. "Should I feel guilty not missing my family and not having chores to do?"

"What for?" Bobby chuckled.

"All because a mysterious metal cylinder inside of space rock falls from the sky. And now I'm thousands of miles from home because of it. Stories like that aren't written in history books; they're fairy tales."

"My whole life is filled with stuff like that."

Caleb looked at him oddly. "Really?"

"I was four years old when I had my first encounter. I was visiting with family in Wonder Valley. It's a place that is not only beautiful, but mysterious and adventurous. I wandered from the house once following butterflies around the field of daffodils. I lost track of where the house was and couldn't figure out which way to go. A pair of goats walked out of the trees and started talking to me."

"Goats don't talk," Caleb reacted.

"That's what my mother said when I told the family about it. But Grandma Rachel argued that it was true. It all started when my great grandparents, Roee and Dodee moved there after Grandpa Roee had an encounter with God in the forest. He was given a special ability to talk with animals. Somehow that gift was given to a herd of wild goats that lived in the valley.

Eventually, everybody moved away, but Grandma Rachel and my grandfather bought a house there after my father left for college. She found the goats were still there. When I went for stay-overs, she'd tell me stories. I was young and I believed them.

"As I got older, I met the goats and they told me stories, too. Then I met the Hunter and everything changed. The extraordinary became ordinary."

"The Hunter." Caleb said thoughtfully. "I can understand how that happens. — What is *your* story with the Hunter?"

"Years ago, while I was visiting the valley, the Hunter started showing me new ideas and mysteries. When I told them to my Dad, he tested them. When he proved them to be workable, he made a name for himself because of it; and made quite a bit of money in the process. We bought our own place in Wonder Valley to be with family and get away from the fame.

"He used the money to build me a really nice sixteen-inch observatory on the property. The fun I had with that encouraged me to follow in his footsteps. And with the money he made, I could afford to be here at Oxford. The Hunter provided for it back when I was just a little kid."

"So, what Doctor Roos said was true." Caleb said with awe. "Your Dad's ideas were actually yours."

Bobby laughed. "I was just the messenger, Caleb. I simply relayed to my father what the Hunter told me. I can't take any scientific credit for that. I didn't even know what I was talking about."

"What's it like having a telescope in your back yard?"

While Caleb asked the question, the professor came in the back door.

Bobby lifted a cup and offered, "Care for some hot chocolate, professor?"

"Tea would suit me, Bobby. — Thanks.

Without further small talk, the professor jumped in, "I've had a brilliant idea, Caleb. Replace Danny while you're here and work for me. It will afford me the luxury of having more time to teach you biblical languages and all that."

Bobby laughed, "And now that you're famous, you can get to know some of the *common* people around campus."

Caleb leaned back and rolled his eyes while the others laughed.

The days ahead were full of study and basketball with Bobby, work and sessions with the professor. Routine settled in while Caleb waited to testify at Anika's trial.

Chapter Twenty-two

Caleb returned to his desk at Professor Sholom's offices after lunch. The professor's morning was busy with lectures and he would be out for a meeting until later. When he sat down, he unlocked the drawer and noticed that the electronic tablet was not in the same position he left it. The doors were locked while he was gone. "So, the professor must have been here," he said to himself. He shrugged, pulled the notebook out and scanned the appointments to get an idea of who and what to expect: Effie Munro at two o'clock and Stanley Farquhar at 3:30. There were no other appointments.

So good, he thought to himself, *we can be out of here by five o'clock.* The last two evenings, the professor had late appointments and Caleb was needed to serve tea and watch the door. And he was happy to do it. His adventure in England was getting better by the day and his time to return home was not established. Conversations with his mom were increasingly focused more on getting back to normal rather than the opportunity he was living. Regular school had been on hold while he was gone, and making up class time was a concern for her. But he was learning to think on levels that provoked a hunger for more. So, normal wasn't something to anticipate. Going back would come before he wanted.

Around 1:15, a woman entered the waiting area and walked up to Caleb's desk. He stood to be polite. But truth-be-told, he was taking mental notes as Holmes and Watson had done. Shorter than Caleb by six inches, about five foot five; average height. She was plain but naturally pretty with minimal makeup. Her loose-fitting brown slacks and tan blouse over a small frame did not attract attention to her figure; dressed modestly. A matching tan cap without advertising blended with her hair color. Lightly tinted glasses hid her eye color. A large bag with a long strap draped over her shoulder appeared to carry a small computer or tablet and doubled as a purse with personal items; perhaps a light jacket for later when it got cool. Nearly everything about her was tasteful but average.

His powers of observation were increasing with practice. Perhaps Mister Holmes and Doctor Watson would be pleased. He also understood the high stakes of letting his guard down. Staying alert and taking note of everything was a constant around the office.

"I'm Effie Munro, and I have a two o'clock appointment. I'm sorry I'm dreadfully early, but I had nothing else to do. Is it okay if I wait? I have some emails to get out."

"Sure Ms. Munro, can I get you anything?"

"What do you have?"

"The usual . . . tea," Caleb returned with an apologetic smile.

"I would be delighted to have a vanilla latte," she sighed.

"The cafeteria has lattes."

"Indeed, it does." She said with a sigh. "If I gave you some money, would you be a good chap and run over and get me a cup?" She lifted her satchel and said, "I would love to finish my work."

Caleb thought about Caitlyn, the lively barista and about this woman; the woman looked trustworthy. "Sure," he responded, knowing the professor would approve of the hospitality. "I have a few minutes. I'd be happy to do it for you."

She handed him a ten-pound note and said, "Get one for yourself as a thank you from me."

"No need, but thanks for offering. It shouldn't take more than ten minutes.”

Heading for the coffee kiosk in the cafeteria, he recalled his brief but pleasant exchanges with the cute barista several times before. She always provoked laughter. Those exchanges kept him returning with hope there would be fewer people, allowing more time to chat with her.

“Hi Caleb,” the cashier had said. “How’s university life treatin’ ya?”

“It’s kind of growing on me, Caitlyn. But I still feel out of place.”

“Ya do look a wee young. But it’s nigh unusual. There are few exceptional young lads around. And ye could pass for one. — So, what brings ya to this illustrious institution?”

Caleb smiled, “It’s top secret. And if I told you, you wouldn’t believe it anyway.”

“We call that nonsense where I come from.”

“Is that in Scotland?”

“Don’t be insultin’,” she stated laughing. “That’s Ireland to be sure.”

Her warmth tugged at a spot in him. He wanted more time with her, but was uncertain how to breech the idea, “Have you heard about the scroll that was stollen and retrieved? It’s been in the news.”

“Of course, Caleb. I knew it was you. But I di’not want to pry where my nose di’not belong.”

Her thoughtfulness touched him. “I would like to talk more, but I need to get back to the office.” Caleb ordered the latte and passed the money to her. She handed him the change and said.

"If ye want some company while yer 'ere, I'd be 'appy to be a friend if ye like."

"I'd like that a lot. I will be off work after five o'clock."

"Weel then, come back 'ere. I'm off at six. We can 'ang about after that."

"If I don't show up, it's because Professor Sholom has delayed me. Would you please come and find me?"

She laughed and stated while concocting the latte, "We Irish are legendary for rescuing the oppressed from their bondage." She rolled the r of rescuing strongly and her pronunciation of bondage sounded like boned age; which got Caleb laughing. "Shall I leave my shield and spear at the door?"

"Oh no," Caleb responded to the banter. "They will be needed to make good our escape. Bring a sword for me," he said holding an imaginary sword in the air. "We shall fight our way out."

She set the lidded latte in front of him with a profound thump and stated, "My battle horse will be waiting at the door, master Caleb. We will make our flight together like clansmen of old."

They talked further until Caleb couldn't ignore the passing of time. As he walked back to the office, Caleb's thoughts were on his growing friendship and how difficult it would be to leave when the time came. He had also taken longer than he said he would, and considered how to word an apology.

Back at his desk, Effie Munro was not in sight. *She probably went to the restroom*, he thought. He set the latte toward the front of the desk, pulled the change from his pocket and put it in the center drawer.

Professor Sholom arrived a few minutes later. The woman with him was talking excitedly using arm and hand gestures to convince him of her point. Caleb rose out of his newly developed habit of taking stock of people and noted her height; shorter than the professor by at least a foot.

The professor addressed Caleb warmly. "How was the afternoon Caleb? I hope you weren't too bored."

Before he could respond, the professor continued.

"Caleb, this is one of my colleagues, Professor Munro. Effie, this is Caleb Hutchins. He's here from the colonies on special assignment. And a remarkable young man with a remarkable story."

"Pleased to make your acquaintance, Caleb," she stated with hand held out.

Caleb took her hand with a pained expression and said, "Professor Sholom, something isn't right here. There was another woman here earlier claiming to be Effie Munro."

Uncertainty filled up the atmosphere until it snapped from tension. "The scroll!" Caleb exclaimed.

He leapt to the professor's door and turned down the lever. There was no resistance and Caleb pushed in.

"Oh no," the professor exclaimed. "That should not be open."

Caleb stood speechless, staring at the open safe. Professor Sholom came up behind . . . The scroll was gone.

"Caleb, do call Mr. Holmes straight away. There is no time to lose. After that, call Scotland Yard."

An hour and a half later, Holmes and Watson strode into Professor Sholom's office, ready for business.

"It is to your good fortune we were in Banbury, Professor. Travel from London at this time of day would have been prohib-
114

itive. I called Lestrade and told him not to bother."

"Now Caleb, start from the beginning and tell us everything. As you know, leave no detail unturned."

Caleb told his story and a detailed description of the woman. The consulting detective and Doctor Watson listened while scouring differing places for evidence and lifting fingerprints. At the end of their investigation, Mr. Holmes left the office to stand at the windows. With his arms folded and chin cupped in his hand, he was lost in meditation pouring over movements, timing and various possibilities. He then put his hands behind his back and paced the length of the room with his chin on his chest. When satisfied with his deductions, he stood before the others and reported.

"I will call Inspector Lestrade and give him my observations. — The woman was a professional and left no evidence. Your general description of the suspect is similar to Irene Adler. Given her skills of deception, she was in disguise; a technique I use on many occasions.

"It is my professional opinion; and I am rarely wrong; that your scroll is no longer in England. Miss Adler sent it by courier to her associates in who-knows-what country moments after leaving the building. Retrieval of it by normal channels will be impossible. — We can only hope it will reappear someday on the black market."

"I apologize for Mister Holmes' cold calculations, Caleb," the doctor stated compassionately while eying Holmes with impatience.

"Ridiculous Watson," Sherlock rejoined. "It is simply the elemental reporting of facts and observations as we know them. If that is too hard to bear," He finished with a cordial bow, "I apologize. I wish I could be more encouraging."

"No need, Mister Holmes," Caleb responded. "My foes are well equipped."

"They can only take your heart," Doctor Watson reminded Caleb, "if you let them. The goods are immaterial."

"Thank you, Doctor," Caleb responded with a nod, a sigh and straightened shoulders. "It's not over until it's over."

"Precisely, Caleb," Doctor Sholom added. "your resolve is admirable. With God's help, I predict a good ending for all this."

Sherlock had been watching the bucking up with interest. "Your confidence in this God of yours may indeed win the day, gentlemen. If that be the case, I may be swayed to believe. Until then, I have only my wits to trust. — And with that, let's be off my good Watson. We have work to do."

"Indeed, Holmes," Doctor Watson responded with a nod. "Good evening, gentlemen."

As they departed, Caleb settled into a chair across from Professor Sholom. They were alone. Professor Munro left with Mister Farquhar when he arrived for his appointment just after Holmes and Watson arrived.

Caitlyn dropped by to find Caleb when he had not shown for their appointed time. He told her what had happened. Sensing his struggle, she sympathized about his loss, and comforted him with a hug. She expressed her excitement of meeting Sherlock Holmes, then departed quietly.

The night looked miserable and murky with disappointment as a fog. But Bobby showed up as self-pity rolled in on Caleb. That downward spiral shifted when Bobby said, "Let's go shoot some hoops."

Chapter Twenty-three

The yellow glow of a sodium yard light was enough to pierce the night's damp fog encroaching on the basketball hoop. It would soon be impossible to see it. Shooting hoops was an attempt to fight back. But pushing back the heavy glum was like trying to push back the fog; it kept rolling in. The scroll was gone for good this time.

Bobby played hard to face Caleb's heavy heart toe to toe. An hour of intense competition pumped adrenaline, trying to work its magic. But like the hand signal for a time out, even heavier fog settled in and made the hoop a shadow. Game paused.

"I'm up for some hot chocolate," Bobby stated breathing hard.

"Might as well," Caleb responded flatly. "We can't see anything in this soup."

Mrs. Sholom thoughtfully left a carafe of hot water waiting with a tea pot and cups. There were options to choose from. Bobby had chocolate prepared in short order and they strolled the hall to the professor's study where the atmosphere was academic, traditional and manly. Whatever came to mind seemed important.

The vintage leather wing-back chairs were untidily arranged near the fire place. Bobby turned on the gas logs as they sat like two politicians considering which global problem to solve. Caleb slouched in his chair with unfolded legs in front of him. He looked around the room while Bobby sat upright watching the flames; his feet raised on an ottoman.

"I love this room," Caleb stated after a couple sips. "It's timeless and rich. It puts me in another dimension — another century; sometime other than now. The ancient stuff wanders within the modern as if to remind us of something. The battles and victories of youth perhaps, coming of age and greatness trying to reveal itself amongst a crowded gallery of potentials."

Bobby tilted his head away from Caleb and squinted. "Are you quoting someone or is that original? That's good insight."

Caleb looked back at Bobby blinking in shock. "It's my own. — I have no idea where that came from." He pondered a moment then added, "Could it be that when something affects you deeply, you see things you didn't see before?"

"You're thinking like an Oxford man, Caleb. It sounds good on you."

"I guess I have changed a bit. I think I observe more. Take this house; it must be hundreds of years old."

"It has a weighty history," responded Bobby. "of high-level conversations of academic and political policy, royal and military decision making; they've all taken place in this room. The Professor has as many stories as the goats back home." Bobby held the cup with his left hand and motioned toward the bookshelves with the other. "If the walls had memory and could talk . . . they would speak of secrets never disclosed."

Caleb nodded as he looked around. "My dad appreciates detail and craftsmanship like the woodwork in this place. He calls it excellence. He says it's a lost art. We remodeled our living room to look a little like this, and I learned a lot about finish carpentry. We took a lot of pride in that project when it was done. But now that I think about it, I wonder if it was really about what we created and how it looked."

"What else could it have been?"

Caleb closed his eyes and sipped his chocolate. "Memories that have meaning. My dad showed me patience and calmness while we worked. We talked about excellence and skill and wisdom and determination to finish a job right. I remember his words, but I'm only beginning to understand what he meant. It's like I have layers. Since I've been here, the problems have peeled back the layers and with each layer removed, I see things differently. And then each layer reveals another layer — I'm not making sense, am I?"

"What about you, Bobby? Do you have a story?"

Bobby gazed at the fire and took a drink. "The institution of Oxford is a thousand years old. Oriel College is only one of several dozen autonomous colleges that make up the university. I could have picked anywhere I wanted to get my PhD. But my dad came here. So, my being here is more about heritage and family, and like you said, even the memories. When my dad came to visit, we were treated like royalty. It's part of the tradition. My dad and I share those things . . . And it will also be a legacy for my children after me, if they choose it. That's important to me.

"My grandma, the uncommon spiritual atmosphere of the valley we live in with its talking goats and angelic visitations, my mother's life of privilege and financial abilities that go back for generations; it's a rich inheritance and filled with stories.

"We could talk like this for a long time, Caleb. I'd rather you got to meet my family and visit my valley. It would add so much more meaning."

"Yeah, I get that. Stories are different than the real thing." Caleb took a bigger gulp now that the chocolate had cooled, then asked, "How long until you finish your PhD?"

"In just a few months I'll be heading back to the states," Bobby chuckled. "Or the colonies as Professor Sholom calls them. I might pick up where I left off with my dad because we love science and we love working together. We make a good partnership.

"My dad says I need to expand my experience, though. And

I've had some amazing offers to work with the best programs available. I just want to finish up here and get home before I decide what to do next."

"You know," Caleb continued in responsive thought, "I've been thinking about what you're doing here to get all this education and degree and stuff, and comparing it with my scroll and how it has brought me here and changed my life. And with that big boulder heading this way that could destroy the earth and all . . . What's the point? Why bother?"

"Those are excellent questions; questions I have asked myself several times. But I found there are more important questions that need answers. 'Why am I here?' and 'What is my purpose in life?' And I can't let the answers to those questions be confused with my earthly assignments and temporary giftings.

"For one, I know I will outlive what's coming whether this body lives through it or not. I have an eternal existence. Jesus died on the cross and rose from the dead to give me that gift. That's what I believe and my hope is that you do as well. — Remember the apocalypse people we talked about?"[1]

"Yeah, they believe the world will crash in some fiery end and we're all going to die."

"It's ignorance Caleb. The world won't end until the work of redemption is complete. It won't be over until Papa God says it's over.[2] It won't be over until Jesus has reigned on earth for a thousand years.[3] What's coming our way is a hiccup in comparison to the massive flameout at the end of time.[4]

"As it stands, I will live through this coming event. I have been told that much by the Hunter. So, I'm moving ahead with my life's long-term earthly purpose. Even if there is a major catastrophe, there will be reconstruction that needs to happen. Then the world will move on in a very different and sober way. And I will be helping in that reformation and making this world a better place by doing my part to bring God's Kingdom to earth.

"But my real purpose during my time here is centered around letting God remake me to have the same amazing qualities of Jesus."

Caleb took it in. But needed help. He wasn't connecting the principle with the circumstance.

"Here's something I don't get, Bobby. God supernaturally gave me that golden scroll . . . And now it's gone. It was stolen on my watch because I wasn't smart enough or man enough to bear the weight of a treasure like that."

"So, you feel like you failed Jesus?" Bobby interrupted.

"Wouldn't *you*?" Caleb stated defensively.

"Yeah . . . yeah, I would. And I honestly feel your pain about it. But I know God. He knew it would happen. And that means he has a bigger plan because he's just bigger than any loss. He's bigger than any failure. He's not mad or upset about it. His purposes are to redeem, recover and restore. You can trust him to make it work for something good, because he *is* good.[5]

"Caleb, you've said before that the real treasure isn't the scroll. You know it's true. If you really believe that, where *is* the real treasure?"

"The answer to that is Jesus," Caleb responded instantly. "Who he is and what he is like, is in the scroll. He's the Word of God. It's the treasure of his Spirit inside us. It's eternal life. It's all good and invisible stuff. It's just that the golden scroll is so . . ." Caleb lifted his hands pulling at an elusive word.

"Tangible?" Bobby finished.

"Yeah, it's worth millions. It's mysterious. It's miraculous. It's the adventure of a lifetime."

"So was the exodus from Egypt. But when it was time to take

possession of the promise, God went after something far more valuable. What do you think that was?"

Caleb felt a ripple down his spine, then sat back and watched the fire. Bobby let Caleb have the space to process. Then Caleb leaned toward the fire and sipped his chocolate. "Everything points toward faith . . . trust. But I could have gotten that at home." He looked at Bobby and asked, "Was my time here wasted? It feels like it was.

"Truth is better than feelings. You were meant to be here. No — you *had* to be here. God moved heaven and earth so you *could* be here. Whatever is ahead, is for you and I to be together doing it. And it was worth this lavish expense for Papa God to make that happen. But he could not allow us to think it was about the scroll and its worth. It has to be different from that because you and I will never be the same because of it. There is something he wants us to understand that is more valuable."

"How will it be different for you, Bobby?"

"Have you ever met someone that you knew was a key person in your life?"

"Not really. But I've never been through anything like this before."

"We started a friendship with Papa God at the center of it. Look at what he's done for you since you've been here. He's set your feet on a path walking in *all* of the Spirit and *all* of the Truth . . . God doesn't want you alone on that path. You were meant to walk it with other people. I'm one of those other people. And I'm looking forward to a *lifetime* of friendship with you and your family, Caleb."

Bobby smiled mischievously. "Stop and think about this, Caleb. This adventure you've been on; the mystery, the intrigue and the famous people." Bobby said with one arm waving. "Win, lose or draw . . . it was worth the excitement. Wasn't it worth getting to experience God on this level? Isn't it worth the stories to tell when you get home? When you have kids? Think about it."

Caleb leaned back in his chair, set the empty cup on the sideboard and smiled. "I wasn't thinking that far ahead. Looking at it like that, yeah, you're right. I don't have the golden scroll, but I have a treasure. I have the pictures and the headlines. I have a story. That's worth something."

Then he stopped suddenly. "If I am to be a world changer, my world and the way I see my world had to go through reentry like a flaming meteor shower."

"A defining moment?" Bobby asked.

"Yeah, a defining moment wrapped in a cosmic event."

"Absolutely brilliant."

Chapter Twenty-four

It was mid-morning. Caleb was with Professor Sholom in his office discussing the Hebrew language. The door was open so Caleb could observe activity in the waiting area. Detective Inspector Lestrade walked up and filled the door opening. He was wearing a trench coat against the moist fog outside and had his hands in his pockets.

With a stiff bow he stated bluntly, "I need a word with you gents."

"Please, come in and have a seat" the Professor responded. "Would you like some tea?"

"That won't be necessary," he said with a wave of his hand. "I will only be a minute."

"What's on your mind, Inspector?"

"It seems that with the loss of the artifact — again — that the evidential backbone of our prosecution of Doctor Roos and Mister Rance, is seriously compromised. The Crown has chosen to direct their efforts on other things. Unofficially Caleb, you will be free to return to the States in short order."

Caleb stood and responded, "That's good news. When will you know?"

"Sometime today. When they give me a written release and ruling, I will pass the release on to you. Your passport will be cleared in the database and you can fly unhindered.

"I was in the vicinity and thought I'd drop in and deliver the news with a personal touch and a word of appreciation from the higher ups for your cooperation." The inspector offered a hand. "Cheers, Caleb. You've been a keen sport through it all, in spite of the rough go we've put you through. Police work and all that."

Caleb took the hand and asked, "When does Doctor Roos get out of jail?"

"She and Mister Rance have been out on bail for some time and were instructed to keep a good distance from you until court time. If you wish to speak with her, you will have to wait until official ruling is handed down."

Caleb nodded with understanding and said nothing in response. His mind flooded with ideas for an unpleasant confrontation. She deserved a piece of his mind. But reality was, the bigger picture had a softer edge. Could she understand that her actions actually worked to gain something with a higher value? He wasn't sure he could explain it.

The inspector pointed a finger. "I've seen that look before, my good man. Revenge will not be tolerated if that's what you're thinking."

"No, sir," Caleb responded defensively.

"See that you don't. — I bid you good day." He pulled up the collar of his coat, turned on his heel and walked briskly away. The room was silent as Caleb sat and watched Lestrade leave.

"I dare say I will miss you, Caleb," Professor Sholom sighed.

Caleb turned to him and said, "That feeling is mutual, professor."

"We will continue our work remotely. This isn't good bye."

"It won't be the same," Caleb responded with a sigh. "But I suppose I will get used to it. — I'm sure my mom will be doing backflips when she hears the news."

Caleb slipped into British speak and stated, "It's all very cheery doing the Oxford bit." Then shifting back to normal, "In some respects, I'm not quite ready for home. I like it here."

"Indeed, Caleb," the professor argued. "There *is* no place like home. I know that sounds cliché. But there is no other step in your adventure to be had here, is there not? Home could be your base to continue this one."

Caleb was uncertain. "I was avoiding thinking that far ahead, professor. Going home will have its challenges."

"I'm afraid I don't see your meaning. What will be your challenges?"

"Being normal," was spoken without hesitation. "I can't go back to what I was."

"Of course. You have changed considerably. You're not the teenage boy you were when you came. Stepping into manhood can be a sticky wicket when your peers don't apprehend the occasion. How *will* you handle your peers?"

Caleb put his hands behind his head, looked up and guessed, "Avoid them?"

"You can't do that, Caleb. They will be looking to you for leadership. — You must give them your humble attention."

"I'm anything but humble," Caleb chuckled. "I'm an Oxford snob now."

"Indeed," Professor Sholom stated. The jest gave him an opening to make a point. "Great opportunity carries great responsibility. The gift you've been given is for the benefit of others. How will you share that gift?"

"Isn't that a big question with a lot of answers?"

"It was meant to be, Caleb. You have a lot to think about when you get home. If you don't, you may find *normal* an attractive comfort for you; an easy life to gravitate toward when you feel alone. You can't allow yourself to go back there. Own your calling and your destiny. Don't let anything sway you from it.

"When you get home, ask yourself the hard questions and answer them. Pray about them. Talk with your father about them. Talk with your mother about them. Keep in mind that you must choose worthy courses of action. And when all your planning is done, let the Lord order your steps."

Caleb felt the weight of the professor's wisdom. "I guess some gifts have to be unwrapped with care."

The professor chuckled, "Or perhaps chiseled from stone."

Chapter Twenty-five

"Gentlemen," Professor Sholom said with enthusiasm. "I'm glad to find you hearth buddies together and in good spirits." He shut the door to the study, rested his briefcase on the desk and turned toward the fire where Bobby and Caleb had been talking. Bobby stood and retrieved another chair; offering the professor his favorite.

"My good Caleb," the professor said as he sat in his chair. "I have excellent news for you. The Oriel College board has set aside a scholarship for you. In addition, we will purchase your ticket home. Perhaps that will set things right for all that has happened."

"My time here hasn't been wrong, professor," Caleb responded. "I've learned some lessons about people I won't forget." Gesturing with his hands; one to Bobby, the other to the professor, he continued, "I've made good friends. And met the kind of characters one only reads about in books. It has been a thought-provoking and heart-rending adventure."

"Not exactly Tom Sawyer stuff," the professor quipped. Bobby laughed.

"Who's that?" Caleb asked.

"A fictional adventurer from the nineteenth century," Bobby accounted. "Along with Huckleberry Finn, they made up the focus of satirical stories as boys coming alive to the social issues of their day."

"I've come alive in places I didn't know needed life. I hope that isn't satirical. By-the-way, what is that?"

"It's like an awakening to the depths of real life in a humorous way," Bobby interpreted.

"Yeah," Caleb reacted. "This has been like — someone took me by the shoulders and shook me hard; definitely woke me up. Maybe someday, I'll find it humorous."

"Yes," the professor added, "you mixed it up with some rough and tumble players on the good as well as the evil sides of your story. Treasures and antiquities attract the smartest of the worst and the best. And I thought Doctor Roos was counted among the best. But the poor thing certainly lost her way over big money. I hope her brush with prison has amended her thinking."

Professor Sholom folded his arms and stretched his legs toward the fire. "And Holmes and Watson; they were intriguing fellows, were they not? Certainly unexpected to have them show up at a time like this."

"I won't forget them," Caleb stated. "Unusual, would be a good description. But I learned a lot from them. Mister Holmes got the job done and didn't let what other people thought of him get in the way."

"Is that a good thing?" Bobby asked.

Caleb shrugged. "It works for him." He chuckled and added, "Maybe not the best of manners and a bit intense. But I can see his logic as a power tool. — My dad would say something like that."

Bobby gave an affirming nod.

"So, what do you think of the scholarship?" the professor asked.

"I don't know if I want to pursue physics, professor. But . . ."

"Nonsense. Undergraduate work doesn't mean you're

committing to physics. It means you're committing to thinking and exploring your options seriously. You'll have tremendous flexibility and I will personally be there to help you along the way."

"Thank you, Professor Sholom. You've surprised me."

"It's the least I could do for you. You have handed me a tremendous treasure."

"I guess I'm feeling unworthy. I lost the scroll . . ."

"That is not the point, Caleb." Using his pointing finger for emphasis, he continued. "These eyes have seen and these hands have held the handiwork of God first hand. It is obviously his. And I am privileged to have beheld it. It is as close to the Ark of the Covenant as any man could want.

"Besides that, I took pictures of the text. I may have been careless with your scroll, but I am not stupid; no indeed. I will spend many blissful hours with the photos I have to work with. And I will send you copies of the digital pictures immediately as well as my translation when it is available. Although I have to tell you, that you are obligated to not go public with any of it for a season."

"No problem, professor."

With that, the professor stood up and headed for the door. "Well, I am famished. Mrs. Sholom says dinner is ready."

"Thank you, Professor," Bobby said shifting to the more comfortable chair. "Caleb and I have one more thing to discuss. We'll be only a few minutes."

"Please don't doddle gents. The Missus will be upset if you let her cooking get cold. Come along."

"We'll talk later," Bobby stated to Caleb.

Chapter Twenty-six

Bobby, Caleb, the professor and Gina were in the driveway sending Caleb off. Bobby would deposit Caleb at Heathrow Airport. Professor Sholom and Caleb shook hands and said farewell. Gina gave the professor a chastising look as an affectionate rebuke for his British stuffiness. She wrapped Caleb in an appropriate hug. The professor responded with a shrug.

"You will always be welcome in our home, Caleb," she stated. "You're a tremendous addition to our family. And I am delighted to have met your mum. She's a champion in my book to have let you do all this. Please give her a hello for me when you see her."

"I will do that, Mrs. Sholom. If it weren't for you, I think she would have lost a lot of sleep. And thanks for the great meals."

"Wait!" Came a cry from the gated end of the driveway. Anika was at the gate waving. Bobby leaned into the car window and grabbed the opener. The gate opened enough for Anika to squeeze through and then closed. After she trotted up, she said, "I'm so glad I made it in time to catch you all together."

The four were silent with uncertainty and their faces showed it. Anika grimaced then sighed and proceeded.

"I cannot adequately express the regret I feel for the embarrassment I put all of you and Oxford through. I brought dishonor to your doorstep and to people I have great respect for. For that I am so very sorry. I let the hunger for wealth corrupt my conscience. It was such a slow slide down that path that I did not realize my condition until I was behind bars. Please believe — that I have seen the dark side and promise not to return to it. — And if I may, I ask your forgiveness."

"I knew you least of all these, and probably least impacted" Bobby responded, "But I see that your sorrow is genuine. I forgive you and hope your future will be as prosperous as the change in your heart."

The professor was next. "From a father's heart, I confess my disappointment, Anika. You're like a daughter to me and my wife. You have been in our home many times. I know you to be a better person than that. I forgive you with this one admonition: please take the time to find out why you were so deceived. What need was so great that you would disregard the well-being of those around you?"

"I will professor," Anika said making eye contact.

"Then I welcome you back to the family without reservation."

"This is hard for me," Gina stated with one hand over her heart. "I can forgive, but it will not be easy to forget. You lived under my roof and ate from our generosity. It is difficult to comprehend what happened to you to betray our kindness this way. Perhaps it is not about us at all; I will grant that. And someday I will understand more than I do now. When you're ready to help me understand, let's have tea and chat face-to-face. Until then — I offer my forgiveness as an act of will and hope my feelings will catch up."

Anika hugged Mrs. Sholom, then stepped back with wet eyes to face Caleb while Gina went back in the house. Caleb looked away, then down, then back to her eyes. She wasn't pleading. But he could tell she was stuck until he spoke. He didn't know what to say. He raised his hands and gave her a crooked smile.

"I know I hurt you, Caleb." Her tears flowed. "What I did to your mother . . . she was my friend. What I did to you; I betrayed your trust and left you alone. And what I took from you . . . is beyond my ability to understand; it was enormous. I will do all I can to make it up to you. I am so, so sorry."

"Doctor Roos, I am sure you weren't thinking about the harm

you would cause. I've done that to my parents before when I wasn't even thinking about the consequences. It's like temporary insanity. So, I can forgive you from experience.

"But honestly, what was meant to harm me, has actually changed me. The value in the golden scroll blinded me to the real treasure inside. And from now on, I'll be careful what I wrap my heart around."

Professor Sholom spoke kindly,

All that is gold does not glitter,
Not all those who wander are lost;
The old that is strong does not wither,
Deep roots are not reached by the frost.

From the ashes a fire shall be woken,
A light from the shadows shall spring;
Renewed shall be blade that was broken,
The crownless again shall be king.[1]

"You will come through this stronger than ever, Anika. And, there is a treasure of hope hidden among these dark and rocky places."

"Yes there is, professor. Thank you." She turned to Caleb, her arms reaching for a hug. After they embraced, she added, "You're a wealthy man, Caleb."

"And he will be a late man for his flight if we don't get going," the professor stated.

On their way, Bobby informed Caleb, "My dad is laying over in Portland at the same time you will be there. I knew about it when I bought your ticket. So, you guys will have a couple hours together."

"Seriously? What do we talk about?"

"He's easy to talk to, Caleb. Golden scrolls, distant galaxies, practical inventions; whatever. You can tell him your story. He's been hearing my adventures for a long time. He'd love to hear something new."

"Planets colliding?" Caleb asked.

"That would probably be a short conversation in public. He wouldn't want people listening in. But if you want to ask about it, go ahead. He'll let you know how he wants to deal with it. And he knows you want to be involved with us. Dad wants you on our team."

"You think things will get nasty?"

"There are people who will make sure it does. And when that time comes, you'll be ready."

Caleb processed through the ticket counter, boarded and settled into his seat. Savoring the opportunity to be alone and think, he pulled out his tablet and checked the charge; ninety-four percent. It had been a while since he played a game. Slipping on the ear buds, he checked the volume.

"It ain't over yet, Caleb." A familiar voice said through the ear buds.

Caleb pulled off the left earpiece, looked at it and smiled. "Hunter?"

Chapter Twenty-seven

Weeks later

Saturday afternoon in the winter outside, while inside life was cozy and warm. Caleb had his back to the wall and sat cross-legged on his bed. He had enjoyed the morning in reflection and reading and now wrote his thoughts. Outside were neighbor-hood sounds of children playing. The distant whimper of a little one and the responding bully from a bigger one told the story of a pecking order being enforced. He remembered those days with a grin; being an only child limited his leverage of telling on those who tormented him. He was always powerless until he got home, where he told his mom everything. She consoled when he was young, but reminded him as he grew that tattling was a super-power not worth using to make himself stronger in his own eyes. It wasn't until his trip to England that he understood where true strength came from.

Mom protected him too much in his estimation. Yet, Dad trained him well in bravery. But since the scroll arrived, his strength training exploded threefold to include God's trans-formational craftsmanship. He faced betrayal, resistance, disappointment, loss and even his sense of justice. And then learned there was a heart position above it all that made him a king. Vulnerability allowed him to serve. Humility allowed him to rule. Taking the hits and staying in the game allowed him to make a difference.

Bobby bought him a journal before leaving Oxford to document this journey and his thoughts about it before the small details faded. The tablet would have worked fine. But something about an actual book felt different. Ink was the blood that flowed from heart to pen, and pages became life.

Conversations and lessons learned, trials and resolutions made, observations and deductions determined; they were all duly written with questions both answered and not. A destiny was handed him. But he wasn't sure what to do with it nor where it would take him. Bobby and Professor Sholom were there to help sort it out and get a grip on what to do. The Word of God and a simple, close life with Jesus kept his focus on who he was doing it for.

And yet, the current chapter of life was just starting. He had been restless and out of sync when he first got home. A few days of Mom's cooking and basketball with Dad restored connection. School work re-centered him. But he missed the personal challenges of England that tried his soul and made him think deep.

It surprised him that it had taken a mere month to catch up on school assignments and then re-pace himself for the regular load. Caleb chuckled. "Now that I have Oxford brains," he wrote, "the work isn't like it was before. I think it has more to do with attitude. But alas, I am caught up. Yay!" He closed the book.

In the classes and halls at school, celebrity status rose and fell in a short-lived and fickle season. He was relieved when his friends discovered he was normal; questions dialed down, gossip less frequent. Say less, laugh more; it was a strategy that contributed to surviving it all.

Yes, something inside had changed. He didn't fit in mainstream school culture. Before England, school was where he was going socially and all that. Now, school was just a *part* of where he was going. He realized there were higher purposes to live for. On peer levels, that kind of thinking was off their radar.

He was having video chats with Professor Sholom. They agreed to resume instruction when he was caught up. He was looking forward to it. He was reading his bible more and having talks with his dad and mom. But the Professor took learning to a richer level.

There were regular conversations with Bobby and occasional

136

talks with Bobby's dad, Richard. The trans-Neptunian planet or asteroid; or whatever it was; was due to appear any day. He wasn't sure what that would cause. With global tension rising, Bobby stepped up his efforts to finish his PhD and get home to be with his father.

Caleb's home front was moving toward its former routine; chores to do, school, friends who wanted to have fun, family that cherished quality time. It was interesting how little time it took to put the scroll and England in the past.

At first, he caught his mom just looking at him. Then she remarked sadly, "You've grown up so much while you were gone, Caleb. I didn't get to watch that happen."

Dad made an off-hand comment after Caleb's return; "Welcome to manhood, son." He had to confess that the experience had him looking at life through different eyes.

Doctor Roos called his mom while Caleb was flying home. Her heart-felt apology made things right with his mom. He didn't know if they would ever see her again. But they would welcome her if she showed up at the door.

A knock on his open bedroom door pulled his mind away from wandering thoughts. He looked up with a wordless response.

"There's a package just come for you," his mom said as she went to the bed and set the box down. "It's got a UK return address."

Dad walked in behind her, saw the box and asked, "What's that?"

Caleb was stumped and said, "I'm not expecting anything." Dad turned to leave. "You can stay Dad. Mom, you too. Enjoy the moment with me—let's see, the return address says 221B Baker Street, London."

"Is that . . ." Dad said smiling as he handed Caleb his pocket knife.

"None other," Caleb interrupted. "It's real Dad. Everything about them is real." Caleb chuckled at a fanciful thought and added, "At least, they were real when I was there."

Caleb pivoted his dad's knife open and scored the tape across the top of the box. He yanked up the flaps and inside was his briefcase. Caleb took the handle and removed it, then shoved the box off his bed.

"It was nice of them to return the briefcase," his mom said quizzically.

"They didn't need to do that," Caleb responded with a scrunched face. "I guess I can put the cylinder parts in it." He flipped the spring latches and opened the lid. On top of the sponge block was a folded note and a manila envelope. Caleb opened the note and read it out loud.

> *My dear Caleb,*
>
> *Once again superior powers of observation and deduction have proven their worth. If I told all, it would be incriminating. So, I shall refrain from revealing certain data.*
>
> *I can tell you with satisfaction the great thrill of being at the scene when a certain nemesis received her due justice. To watch Mister Holmes patiently and skillfully out-wit the woman is a memory that will last the duration of my lifetime.*
>
> *With gratifying pleasure, we forward to you the fruits of our*

labors. Need I remind you of the discretion needed to possess this treasure? Nonetheless, it is yours and you will handle it as you wish.

On behalf of myself and Mister Sherlock Holmes, we dare say it has been the grandest pleasure to have known you and been a small part of your adventure.

Sincerely now and forever yours, JW on behalf of SH

PS: Much indebted to the assistance of Doctor Anika Roos. She has redeemed herself from her former status.

PSS: The other envelope is from Professor Sholom.

"John Watson on behalf of Sherlock Holmes?" Dad exclaimed with a British accent. "That's extraordinary."

"Time and space leave little reasonable explanation for it, my dear Dadson." Caleb stated in mimic Sherlock. They laughed in response.

"So, what's in the envelope, Caleb?" his mom wondered.

"The envelope?" Caleb pushed on the sponge. His eyes grew expectant while he removed the spilt top. The golden gleam of his treasure had returned home. He smiled and remembered Doctor Watson's pledge: *Rest assured, we shall stand with you also, whenever and wherever it is needed.* Grateful for the best of key players providentially put in his path, his heart overflowed. Heroes still exist; good people doing good without thought for themselves.

That night as he lay on his bed in the dark, questions mounted.

Was all this adventure uniquely crafted by God for my benefit? Would he do this for the pleasure of us having time together? Would he move heaven and earth like that to show me his love? . . . years before I was born? Centuries of time? . . . Before time? And concerning Holmes and Watson, *out of time?*

A glow kindled at the desk where Caleb did his studies. The scroll was open with a mist forming around it that spread. Caleb watched. Peace filled the atmosphere.

"I get it, Lord . . . Yes, you would."

In the excitement of the returning scroll, he forgot about the manila envelope. He switched on the light and retrieved it from the desk. Inside was a certificate with the Oriel College Crest surrounded by swirling calligraphy and Oxford University heading. It was signed by the regents and said,

Caleb Hutchins

is hereby bestowed the honorary title of

Surpassing Englishman

With all benefits, privileges and rights

to be

granted in perpetuity.

Caleb laughed. He would frame it as a fond memory and hang it where he could see it always.

Chapter Twenty-eight

Caleb paced, waiting for Bobby to answer the call. When Bobby's face appeared, Caleb injected, "Hey Bobby," his voice elevated. "You won't believe what happened yesterday!"

Bobby smiled and responded, "It must be good, you're pumped. What happened?"

With hands on his hips, Caleb waited, shaking his head. Then he leaned toward the camera with a broad smile and stated in slow cadence, "I got the golden scroll back." After his announcement, he brought the scroll up for Bobby to see.

Bobby jumped out of his chair, punched a fist in the air, shouted "Yeah," then pumped two fists in front of his chest, saying, "That's fantastigorical, Caleb!"

Caleb grew a lopsided grin. "That's a real word?"

"It is now. I'm getting a PhD; I can make up stuff." As they laughed Bobby continued. "Well come on, tell me about it."

"Doctor Watson sent it with my briefcase. I don't know how they did it, he couldn't say anything in his note. I'll have to call and find out. However it was done," he stated with arms flung wide, "it had to be masterful. And get this, Doctor Roos *helped* them get it back."

Bobby was thoughtful. "It's beautiful to see her regret put into action. That's the real thing. And Holmes and Watson — they know how to get the job done. I definitely want to hear the rest of *that* story."

"Oh yeah," Caleb responded. "We'll be sworn to secrecy, I'm sure. I definitely won't say anything publicly; I don't want people to know I have the scroll back.

"Have you called Professor Sholom?"

"He's next. I had to call you first and get you to design a vault for this guy that can take a direct hit from an asteroid." They chuckled and Caleb continued. "I'm not afraid of losing it as much as I'd like to avoid the weirdness it invites. I want a wall between me and those people."

"People will want to see your scroll, Caleb. It's as mysterious as the holy grail. I don't envy your possession of it. You should ask the Hunter; he'll tell you what to do. After all, he knows where the ten commandments are kept."

"Yeah, there's a good idea."

The conversation stalled as the subject closed down. Caleb stepped outside the view of the camera and lay down the scroll. Upon return, he asked, "Well, that's my latest news. — What's going on with you? How's your dad?"

"You picked the perfect time to call, Caleb. We've been talking about you." Bobby shifted in his chair and faced Caleb squarely. "We need your help."

"You got it. What can I do?"

"The asteroid has cleared the sun; we have access to it now. Most of our analysis is complete with minor bits still being calculated."

"Is it serious?"

"It is. The official classification is a Near-earth Object with a Potentially Hazardous designation. Its elliptical shape looks a lot like Haumea with a big chunk knocked out of it. For the sake of the public mind, we are simply calling it an asteroid. Giving it a name makes it more like a monster than an object."

"I don't know anything about Haumea or any of that other stuff. Is it going to hit earth?"

"Haumea is a dwarf planet that is shaped like a football. Our asteroid is like it; rolling end over end. Current calculations tell us that one end may be pointed at the planet when it passes by. Fortunately, it won't be a direct hit. But having that end dip inside the atmosphere makes unknown variables highly possible."

"How big is it?"

"Big enough to terrorize the entire population of planet earth. It's smaller than the moon on the pointy sides of it and larger in the middle. That makes it the biggest space object to pass by our planet in recorded history. It's gravitational effects on our planet will create huge problems. But the good news is, critical mass will only last a few seconds. It's moving fast.

"But what we need right away is special people who can keep a cool head under pressure and help us prepare for what is coming. I believe God has prepared you for this time. Will you step up to the plate and help us face this?"

"I don't know if I'm as fearless as the job calls for, Bobby."

Bobby stood and changed the camera position. His hands helped to convey the importance of his words. "I'm not asking you to be fearless, Caleb. What we're facing is unavoidable. But I know you. You won't quit. You won't give up, even when you feel like it. That's what I'm asking for. That, and a willingness to meet with scientists, world leaders without being intimidated and tons of people from our generation. You will need to respectfully and honorably explain the enormity of the situation and the steps we have designed to prepare for the times. And of course, you will have to face a media that is making a story rather than presenting the truth."

"Yeah," Caleb said thoughtfully. "Man." He folded his arms and looked sideways toward Bobby. "Are you sure you got the right guy? I'm just a kid."

"You're no ordinary kid, Caleb. You're a world changer. And you'll be working with my dad as an ambassador of information and technology as we talk about solutions for this problem and its aftermath." Bobby chuckled and added, "You'll learn how to communicate with all kinds of people — if you live through it."

"Wow, Doctor Bobby," Caleb said with raised eyebrows. "That's encouraging. When do we start?"

Bobby smiled. "As soon as you stop calling me Doctor. But I want to be real; it will likely get hostile. — Can we contact your school and let them know you're needed?"

"Okay . . . Is talking to my parents on your list of things to do?"

"Are they home?"

Chapter Twenty-nine

Twenty-five months later

Those extremely exhausted from the constant vigil found sleep on cots while the control room stayed connected to all outposts around the globe. It was morning, and realities regarding the end of the day made little difference rested or tired. In retrospect, most *business as usual* thoughts had been discarded with the passing of the last two years. Future as a calculated pursuit had been laid to rest for the sake of the current peril. Doomsayers proclaimed a cataclysmic end of all things. Optimists, on the other hand, had grand ideas for tomorrow's genesis. Regardless of various facts and opinions, planet earth would not be the same by sundown.

"We are approaching zero hour with this asteroid, Doctor Kromberg," the news anchor pointed out. "What would you have to say at this time about the collision course we are on?"

"According to our best calculations," Bobby shared seriously to the cameras, "we are not on a collision course. This asteroid's impact on earth is a fact of proximity. We have done all we can to predict gravitational influences of a spinning, elliptical object and what could unexpectedly happen as it goes by us so fast and so close. Yes, scientifically speaking, the after-effects range from minimal to catastrophic. But I have to be clear, there is simply no way of knowing everything in certainty."

He turned to the anchor and continued, using his hands to express himself. "As you know, we've been aware of this asteroid for the better part of fifteen years and we have prepared as much as anyone could for something of this magnitude. The entire world followed our efforts to inform and prepare for this moment. Obviously, a near miss is a far better scenario than the holocaust of a collision. But let me say this: what time we have while waiting to see what the outcome of this will be, should be spent in the comfort of faith, hope and love."

The anchor argued, "Doctor Kromberg, you sound resigned to some predetermined fate; kumbaya and all that. Certainly, with all the computing power you have available, can't you do better than that? Isn't there something more you can do?"

"There are too many variables to be precisely accurate," Bobby responded, letting his irritation leak out. "We have *not* created a false optimism with *anyone* at *any* time in making that point."

The anchor smiled slyly; the button he was looking for revealed itself. He pushed it. "Isn't it true, Doctor Kromberg, you're being vague to prevent a global panic? You owe the world the truth. This is history in the making and the record keepers of this planet will hold you responsible for your dishonesty. Do you want that as your legacy?"

Bobby calmed his reaction to being baited before responding. "I am not lying or remotely being vague, Mister Fray. We have objectively reported everything science has provided. I refuse to establish in anyone's mind that ignorant speculations or exaggerated fairy tale endings as fact. One thing I know by faith; it won't be the end of the world."

"That's hypocrisy Doctor. You refuse ignorant speculations and so-called fairy tale endings. Yet, you want the world to buy into religious rhetoric. It's all the same story. There's plenty of nut cases on street corners around the globe proclaiming judgement and how much we deserve what's coming. Do you really expect people to fall for this self-righteous drivel?"

"You're not hearing me, Mister Fray," Bobby spoke impatiently. He was tired, and tired of Fray's twisted moderation. He spoke boldly and plainly, "I'm begging everyone to turn to the only hope *anyone* can possibly count on. Jesus will see us through this crisis. *Call on him!*"

Fray turned to the camera. "There you have it, folks. Another stanza of "He's Got the Whole World in His Hands," sung for you at the height of an astronomical crisis by Doctor Bobby Kromberg. Don't count on any help from heavenly headquarters. Barbara, back to you for the wrap."

The reporter didn't bother to thank Bobby as the feed returned to the main anchor where opinion, bias and drama would have the last word. Bobby walked off shaking his head. He rejoined his dad, friends and the global crisis command crew, where clearer heads were focused on executing what solutions they had.

Caleb stood with his own dad watching the bank of monitors with a concerned look as Bobby walked in. He turned and said, "I hope we've done enough, Bobby."

"You too, Caleb? Are you doubting that God will make this work for good?"

Caleb felt the weight on Bobby's shoulders and asked, "What happened with the media peeps?"

Bobby sighed then combed his hair with his fingers, leaving his hands intertwined behind his head. "The news people are determined to blame somebody for what can't be helped. Their minds are resolved to story mongering. They're irrational, and unreasonably manipulating the narrative to agitate emotions. It's a tough filter to get through."

"And it's just irritating?" Caleb added looking at the floor and folding his arms across his chest.

"It's politics and posturing for attention at the lowest levels of humanity, Caleb." David stated, hands on his hips.

Bobby responded before Caleb took a breath. "It's all that, David, and more. There's unseen forces at work to keep people focused on the problem and not the protector." Bobby sighed. "What have you told Caleb since he was a kid?"

David put his hands in his pockets and looked up mentally reviewing a list. "It ain't over until it's over, for one thing. It's a quote by a baseball coach from way back."

"It *ain't* over," Bobby exclaimed with both arms raised. "Something different is about to happen; something good. God brings creative redemption from chaos, and beauty from horrific ash heaps. You see it in the Bible and in history. Pulling this off to perfection isn't our job. Fighting the battles of faith and truth *is* our job. As we keep going and never give up, we get to see marvels and miracles wrap around the impossibilities."

"I agree," David rejoined. "You may have a long road ahead of you and I may not. But finishing well is *my* goal, thanks to the makeover I've seen God work inside Caleb. You've all held your course under intense fire. You haven't waivered. You've been a huge example to me. I never thought being a Christian could be this intense and exciting. I'm a tradesman, I find pleasure in working with my hands. Now I get to work with God the master builder. I'm staying until he's done all he can do with me. Wherever that takes me, I'm in.

"And guys, listen, you haven't failed. I agree, that this event is a turning point. We will make the turn and keep going, create the future and face our enemies. And Bobby, I understand how you feel about carrying the weight of responsibility. You knew about this in advance, and you wanted to be a part of the solution. But the end game doesn't begin until this is over. We can't settle in and regroup until we're on the other side of it."

"Thanks for your encouragement, David." Bobby added. "Having you and Caleb with us means a lot to me and my dad. Having your love amongst all the fear has made the tension bearable. There were moments we needed heavy support and you guys gave it. And personally," Bobby turned to Caleb, "I just needed to step away occasionally and shoot hoops with a friend."

Caleb nodded his head and replied, "I remember when someone did that for me." Caleb returned eye contact. No more words were necessary.

Their attention returned to the large-screens. As they watched, the sky turned dark in some of the monitors as tribes and families worldwide watched satellite feeds focus on the incoming asteroid now eclipsing the sun.

Twenty-four large screens at the NASA space center in Houston, Texas monitored the global situation. Computer mock-ups of the asteroid's trajectory with gravitational corrections were displayed alongside virtual graphics projecting hopeful outcomes.

"It's moving fast," Bobby said to Caleb. "It will be over in a matter of seconds."

"What's the biggest variable in your calculations?" Caleb asked. Variables became a catchword through the months of talks with nations and scientists. It was a constantly changing measurement and Caleb was assigned to updating his peers regularly on what they were and, to the best of anyone's understanding, what they meant.

"Gravitational pull mostly. Mass, tumble and speed are big ones. And the unpredictability of what effect the earth's gravity will have on it gives us just a hint of where it's going once it passes by. Great or small, the beast will undoubtedly change trajectory.

"It's a boulder the size of California and Oregon in diameter, acting like it's tumbling downhill. The tumble increases as it gets closer and moves faster. As it enters the atmosphere, it will heat up. We can closely calculate how that will affect the rock and how the rock will affect the atmosphere. We have a hundred educated analysts trying to figure the broader picture. But like your dad said, we will have to recalculate everything when it's over."

"Won't there be a slingshot effect?" David asked.

"Not like the slingshot effect used to change a spacecraft's trajectory and increase its speed into deep space. Yet, to be honest with you, a few people have been concerned enough about it to work the possibilities. But it's way heavier than a spacecraft and moving many times faster. I think we shouldn't be bothered by it. — If it actually bumps earth? . . . Well, we'll see if that happens."

"We have a visual," was the announcement on the sound system. It was Bobby's dad, Richard. "The estimated time of arrival is five minutes. Projected location of pass-by is the Pacific Ocean. Triangulation puts it somewhere inside the Christmas Islands, Marshal Islands and Hawaiian Islands."

"Oh Jesus, help us," Bobby prayed.

"Isn't that a good thing?" Caleb asked. "The map shows there's no land masses out there."

"True, but that's deep ocean. Even a small part of that monster hitting deep water will create a tsunami big enough to devastate every coast on every continent along the Pacific Rim. And the islands won't stand a chance."

The next minutes were intense and prayerful.

The public address system crackled, "Increase frame-rate on one of the feeds to accurately capture location and give slow motion capabilities."

"Got it, good idea," Richard responded. "Thank you."

"Who said that?" Caleb asked out loud. "That voice is familiar." Eyes turned to look for a hand to go up.

"Caleb," Bobby said excitedly. When Caleb turned to him in response, Bobby was smiling. Then he pointed to a cubicle on the other side of the large room where a man in camo-wear sat looking at them. His face was peaceful and confident, yet sadness was there, too. He used two fingers to point to his eyes, followed with two pointing at them. "I am with you," he mouthed without speaking.

Caleb and Bobby looked at each other as a calm enveloped them. When they looked back, the Hunter had disappeared. But he certainly hadn't left.

As the rock entered the atmosphere, video feeds went dark as satellites were destroyed. What the ground cameras captured looked horrifying as the rock filled the eastern sky in blazing speed then disappeared. Where one feed left off, another picked up until it went over the Pacific Ocean. The explosive concussion of sound-breaking speed was enormous; even shaking the building.

On the other side of the Pacific, cameras continued until the asteroid left the atmosphere. More cameras went dark. The pass-by was over.

Cheers rose to heightened pitch in the command room in Houston as two years of tension found a release. Some danced, some shouted and some sat pensively shedding their burden.

Bobby and Caleb smiled.

"Let me have your attention, please," Richard announced on the intercom and to the extended global support network. His voice was serious and he sounded exhausted. "Although a direct hit did not happen, pictures indicate that the sonic concussion created enough pressure to indent the ocean water for thousands of miles. Exact measurements will be short-coming.

An update came two minutes later: "Tsunami sightings are coming in from ships at sea. Shipping tonnage has been lost as well. Emergency plans have been activated for the Pacific Rim. Unfortunately, loss of life is expected. Stand by for details. If you are a member of an emergency team, be prepared to hear from your team leader and respond quickly."

A few minutes later Bobby and Caleb were standing at the monitors watching the computer rendition of the rock's projected flight path and the slow-motion replay of its real time event as it passed by. Caleb looked at it quizzically and turned to Bobby.

"Hey Bobby, uhh, what do you make of that projection of the flight path?"

Bobby looked up, his mouth dropped some, his face went serious. "That's two dimensional, it may not mean anything. Let's check with the eyes-in-the-sky people and see if they have any visuals on it." He keyed the microphone near his mouth. "Can somebody get me a 3-D rendering on screen twelve, please?"

Bobby looked to the glassed-in command center and got his dad's attention by hand-waving him. He pointed two fingers at his eyes then one finger at Richard, then one finger at the feed. It took just seconds to understand what was about to happen. Richard raised his hands in helplessness and yelled, "*What next!*"

"Caleb," Bobby said, "in just a few minutes, the moon as we know it will be history."

Caleb and Bobby watched and waited. The crash sent two celestial bodies reeling like melons smashing. The impact shattered the asteroid and split the moon into pieces major and lesser. Some people in the room flinched involuntarily, others ducked or hunched their shoulders.

What all this meant now sent another wave of perplexity reeling in each scientific mind and heart. In Caleb, it formed a question.

"What are we going to tell the world about this, Bobby?"

"We tell them it ain't over. We tell them not to give up. We tell them it's time to get to work and restore what we have."

"What does that look like?"

"It looks like hope and creativity, Caleb. With God, anything is possible."

"Most of the world doesn't understand that language; it's beyond human ability." Caleb considered the journey he'd been on since receiving the golden scroll. Had it not been for that event, he would not have been equipped for this one. Human need will be looking for solutions on scales beyond comprehension. "This is your time, Bobby. You're the solutionary. You see and know things beyond human knowledge. Between us and our dads, we have a great team to work with. Where do we start?"

Chapter Thirty

Four days later

"It was a no-brainer press release. But NASA required us to officially report the asteroid as a near miss for their archives." Doctor Richard Kromberg led the discussion of the online group meeting. The participants were most of the emergency team leaders throughout the world. Bobby, David and Caleb were with him, bunched close at the table with camera and microphone as centerpieces.

The meeting was led from the dining room at the Kromberg estate in the serene settings of Wonder Valley. Yet even with the valley's beauty and peacefulness, the mood around the table was subdued. The moms and Grandma Rachel were outside praying.

Richard delivered his presentation focused on his electronic tablet. "Although the announcement downplayed reality, the effects of the asteroid can't be marginalized. The event was hugely devasting and, as you already realize, the fallout from it is mounting."

"Our latest report is in alignment with what our experts are saying. The moon's gravity created tension on Earth's tectonic plates as well as high and low tides for the oceans. Without that tension, parts of the planet are settling into new positions with grim consequences and without tide movement ocean currents are slowing. It will be years before this planet finds its new normal." Richard looked at the camera and added, "Folks, planet Earth has not been down this path before."

A text appeared on the screen from a team leader, *Not that we know of* ☺.

The guys chuckled, causing Richard to look at the screen. He smiled, shook his head, gave a thumb up and went back to his prepared text.

"During this period, expect earthquakes to be a way of life. Building permanent structures will require new levels of engineering. Power grids and other utilities will have to be redesigned with flexibility in mind. Global navigation will be a nightmare as the magnetic poles move around. A host of other projected problems will arise and undoubtedly, more than a few that cannot be predetermined; they will simply show up.

"The latest group wanting attention is the mental health people. I'm not going to go into detail. But your governments need to be aware and plan. Expect long term uncertainty and fear to have a toll on the well-being of your populace. Should that be a surprise?"

Although vocal responses were muted, nodding heads showed affirmation. Texts appeared on the screen in one form or another stating, *Makes sense*.

Richard looked to David. "David, this would be a good time to share your report."

David tapped his tablet. "On the day the asteroid passed by, tsunamis destroyed a third of the ships at sea in the Pacific as well as those harbored around the Pacific Rim at the time. Losses of commerce and life on land and sea are beyond calculation. Indicators are, that as much as a third of the earth will be ruined economically and ecologically.

"My understanding of this next thing is limited. What I've been told is that the asteroid super-heated as it blazed through Earth's atmosphere, burning off bitter toxins that are still falling. Life in the Pacific and in fresh waterways is perishing along the path of the asteroid. With earth's rotation, changing weather patterns, storms and water-spouts, contaminants are getting into municipal water supplies. People are dying from drinking polluted water.[1]

"Clean water is already a major issue. But what is going on along the asteroid's path is expected to grow. We're counting on those nations unaffected to lend a hand. Please contact me if you can help so I can focus your efforts to where it is needed. There are other agencies taking care of food and medical. If you have specific questions about that, send me an email." David gave Richard a nod that he was done.

Richard sighed. "I wish there was more to be said that was even slightly positive. Environmental circumstances have been set in motion that simply must run their course before they get better. Any fresh ideas can be run through Caleb." He recapped the main issues, gave the leaders instructions for follow-up and closed the online meeting.

"There is some growing hope," Caleb said. "I have people wanting to collaborate ideas and look into the efforts of those who prepared well to help reconstruction. And the number of disaster volunteers are growing. Hopefully the message of inter-dependence won't get shouted down and shoved aside."

Bobby raised a finger. "I have a concern . . . Opportunists have found a rallying point, and they're demanding to be heard. Those voices are directed at us. They want us arrested and prosecuted for crimes against humanity." Bobby let the impact settle in. Heads shook.

"I know . . . it sounds stupid and ignorant.

"These are a small minority of citizens stirring up unrealistic issues with us. But the reality is they have no authority to act. Although we are legally protected, they've been given a microphone by the media and they're reaching vulnerable nerves that are willing to go along with the delusion. We need to be extra careful in public settings. Dad especially you, since you were on the front line when the story broke. It's your face that represents their grievances. I hope you will consider getting a bodyguard or two."

Richard sighed. "That's a decision I'm not ready to make,

Bobby. Having bodyguards is like telling people we're afraid. I don't want to encourage that. And don't forget that you've been with me on that front line for a lot of years. You're a target by association."

"Dad, I don't want to see anything happen to you," rejoined Bobby, downplaying his dad's concerns.

Richard smiled, but his eyes didn't. "I know you have bigger angels watching over you, but my little ones will work just fine. — Look, I appreciate your concern. But I'm not going to do anything at this time. I don't want that kind of attention." His face softened and he added, "But, for your sake, I'll think about it. — What about solutions, Bobby? Anything on the horizon?"

"I've put out questions to help me analyze what's happening out there. But I've had little time to get deep into the nuts and bolts." Bobby sat back in his chair and wove his hands behind his head. "That's why we're all here, so *we* can take the time and talk about it. Let's step away from crisis management and political obstructions to look forward; let's get ahead of this."

"I'm sorry Bobby, David and I need to get back at the wheel of the crisis helm. We don't have the luxury of everybody doing the same thing. You and Caleb will have to do some navigating and find a course for us."

"Between us and the Hunter," Caleb rejoined, "we'll get it done."

Richard grasped Caleb's shoulder. "I'm counting *heavily* on that."

Chapter Thirty-one

The sun had set behind the mountains moments before. And now the azure sky silhouetted the forest on their peaks who pointed at the gold and red cloud cover floating motionless above them. The tranquil beauty was overlooked by the noise of a dribbling basketball.

"I don't get their thinking!" Caleb said loudly. Another shot swished through the hoop net. "*We* didn't destroy the moon." Bobby rebounded the ball then dribbled a short distance from the backboard while listening. He took a shot.

"How could it possibly be our fault?" He asked, jogging forward to recover Bobby's shot. "Did *we* send that crazy asteroid to pick it off? No! How can people blame us for what happened?"

"As strange as it seems," Bobby said with a wag of his head and outstretched hands, "there are lots of people who don't have the same mind as we do."

"Duh, you don't say," Caleb howled sarcastically as he cleared another hoop. "Is *that* why we have wars?"

"The world is on edge, Caleb. Security has staggered and fallen like a drunk. The moon that stabilized the earth and reacted with it to form some level of predictability is broken.[1] And the natural order is searching for another expression. And you can guarantee that the defeated side of our spiritual realities is trying to use the chaos to get a foothold." Bobby quit dribbling and took a shot. It hit the rim and ricocheted back to him. He grabbed it and passed it to Caleb.

"Look, rational people know it isn't our fault. But it's the people who are captivated with fear that are screaming the loudest. The world isn't rational to them. They're victims to it and need a bad guy to vent on.

"And hear another perspective to that; their fears are being exploited. It's to the profit of the drama mongers in the media to sell stories that keep people worked up and staying crazy." Bobby jumped and retrieved a missed shot by Caleb.

"Common sense will return when people are done with their addiction to that stuff. — And you've got to know it didn't help us when that hot asteroid dumped its' bitter fairy dust on the planet. But the reality is, it's internal bitterness about life gone haywire that is killing people.[2] This chaos is creating unstable and pliable minds that are willing to believe anything that artificially sounds like hope.

"There's a lot of propaganda targeting confused and hurting people to buy into misdirected agendas. It's false narrative about all that is wrong on this planet; governments, structures, cultures, religion. And for now, the enemies of that narrative happen to include us. As illogical as it seems, their rhetoric has determined that if the bad guys of faith are eliminated, justice will be served, everything will be made right and all will be well again. Then they will come out of it looking like leaders of a new movement. And who would dare resist?"

Caleb responded, "History paints a tragic portrait for the end of that line of thinking, Bobby. Social upheavals get started. Opinion becomes the measure of right and wrong instead of truth. People of differing ideas, truth, justice and faith die in the streets or get shipped off to concentration camps."

"Honestly Caleb, what you're saying sounds like additional drama," Bobby responded. Then he realized he had invalidated Caleb's observations. "Yeah, there is historical reality to it. But I don't want to die for discovering a cosmic event and being helpless to stop it; what a waste. Good people were burned at the stake during the Dark Ages by people blindly believing twisted logic like that. Millions of innocent and unsuspecting people have died at the hands of monstrous sociopaths during times like this. It staggers my mind to watch people follow deceiving wolves in sheep's clothing and ignore the truth.

"Did you know that while chaos spreads over a third of the earth, increasing numbers of leaders and speculators are calling for a restructuring of geopolitical factors on a global basis? Many countries along the Pacific rim are now collapsed economies because of what has happened. A uniform world order would relieve these governments and rescue their people. It's a setup, Caleb."

Caleb was quiet and didn't respond. His friend was ranting about something that went deeper than the words he was hearing. They continued to shoot and rebound, but Bobby's face showed the weight of something he hadn't resolved.

Caleb grabbed a rebound, dribbled then stopped. With the ball stuffed in the crook of his arm, he faced Bobby. "Why are we talking about death and revolution? This isn't like you. All this negativity is sucking the oxygen out of the air."

Bobby felt Caleb's loving blast of honesty. His statement blew away the smog and he realized he wasn't in a good frame of mind. "You're right, Caleb. — We need some hot chocolate."

Caleb smiled. "This sounds like a three-cookie conversation."

Bobby laughed. "I hope we have some cookies."

Bobby made chocolate while Caleb checked the cookie jar. "It's empty."

"Check the pantry. Dad always has Oreos around."

Caleb came back with a package of double stuff Oreos. "Mission accomplished." He opened and shut several cabinet doors before finding a suitable bowl and put half the package in it.

Bobby looked at Caleb then the bowl and said, "They're small cookies, right?"

Caleb lifted one to the front of his face. "They're *good* cookies." He stuck the whole thing in his mouth and smiled.

Bobby shook his head. "Why don't you go fire up the pellet stove and pull a couple chairs together. I'll be right there."

Caleb mumbled something through his full mouth, took the bowl and headed for the living room. The pellet stove was similar to the one at home, so he lit it without a problem. The chairs were already in place. He positioned an end table between them and landed the cookies as if the bowl was a space ship. Then sat heavily, slouched down and crossed his legs at the ankles. He was ready.

Bobby brought the mugs, took in the scene and handed Caleb his chocolate. He sipped his brew then set it next to the bowl of cookies. He went behind his chair and leaning on the back, folded his arms.

"There *are* solutions to the mounting problems of not having a moon. But the enemy's scheme is to distract us from our assignment. By keeping us focused on less important questions, Papa God's Kingdom advancement is being sabotaged. And the false accusations and threats on our lives — Yeah, it's dirty politics. And because of it, I was forgetting to trust God."

Bobby sighed, changed to the front, settled back in his chair and looked at the ceiling. "If I had a workable solution, I'd be willing to die for *that*."

It dawned on Caleb what had been bothering Bobby. "You're pretty sure you're going to be martyred for your faith."

"I don't want that to happen before I get my assignment accomplished. All this resistance is keeping me from figuring things out. And the spiritual atmosphere is getting more hostile with each new day. It concerns me that I don't have any answers."

Caleb stared at the slow-dancing flames on the other side of the glass in the pellet stove as he pondered their dilemma. He felt useless. Another asteroid to take the moon's place was the best his imagination could grasp so far. It wouldn't happen by chance; it had to be a precisely engineered event.

Caleb's gaze was drawn to the large picture windows on the other side of the pellet stove by movement in his peripheral vision. His leaned forward and swept the surrounding land-scape. An animal was partially hidden behind a patch of manza-nita, grazing leisurely on nearby foliage.

"Bobby, what kind of animal is that?"

Bobby got out of his chair and walked to the window. He smiled broadly and said, "I know who that is, Caleb. I haven't seen any of them since I was a teenager. And where there's one, there are others."

Bobby turned to Caleb and declared, "Caleb, have I got a surprise for you."

Without another word, Bobby grabbed some cookies, turned and opened the sliding glass door. Caleb followed with, "You think it'll spook and run? Are they friendly?"

Bobby didn't answer, and walked briskly toward the goat. It turned its head and said while it chewed and swallowed, "Good evening, Bobby. An angel sent me to meet with you. My tribe sends you and your grandmother greetings."

Caleb's jaw dropped and Bobby laughed and exclaimed, "I love it when you guys show up when I'm lost and need help. Here, have a cookie."

"Thanks. — You mean the moon thing," the goat said casually. "That was an amazing sight."

"What's your name?" Bobby asked. "It's been years since the last time I saw you guys. I don't remember any names or faces. — But where are the others? You guys never travel alone."

"My name is Scampy. I was told to come alone and talk to you."

"I heard about you from Grandma Rachel. You don't look that old."

"I was named after my great-grandfather; an extraordinary goat of great faith that led the flock during the Ruction; the great upheaval. He knew little Rachel and her Mama and Papa before they moved away. The tribal stories about them are still being told, you know. We still run into Mama Rachel when she's out walking, but we miss not having little children around. Where are your children?"

Bobby laughed. "I don't have any yet, Scampy. Papa God needs to do something, or they may not have their day. There's a lot of people that want to kill us for killing the moon. And I'm at a loss about what to do."

"Why not create a new one," Scampy said plainly.

Bobby looked at Caleb with a smirk and questioning eyes.

"Oh yeah," Caleb responded affectionately. He raised a wagging finger and finished, "I was about to suggest the same thing, Bobby."

Bobby rolled his eyes, shook his head and turned to Scampy. "Okay Scampy. You apparently see something I'm missing. Tell me more."

"It's so simple, a goat could do it. The great hunter of souls, Jesus, says that if you have faith in your heart the size of a mustard seed, you can tell a mountain to move out of your way and you will see it move. There is nothing you couldn't do."[3]

"You have seen the Hunter?" Caleb asked in a wave of curious. "What does he look like to you?"

"Of course we know the Hunter. He lives in these mountains and this valley." Scampy responded matter-of-factly. "But you distract me from my point. Please listen."

"I'm sorry, Scampy. It's just that I have seen him and talked with him."

Scampy looked at Caleb blankly. "Yes, that is normal."

Caleb recognized that he had derailed Scampy's thinking. "So, you were talking about faith like a mustard seed. And what the Hunter says about it. Don't you mean that he *said*, not he *says*?"

"Not at all," Scampy defended sharply. "Whatever he said, he is still saying. The Hunter is always the same, nothing's changed. — Now, if you will be so kind as to not interrupt, I was saying; not said."

Caleb nodded. "Go ahead."

"I don't know what a mustard seed looks like, but it can't be bigger than a gnat or a fly. That ain't much. Just grow it a little bit more and you could create a moon."

"He also says that if you have the smallest measure of authentic faith, it would be powerful enough to say to a large tree, 'My faith will pull you up by the roots and throw you into the sea,' and it will respond to your faith and obey you."[4]

Bobby and Caleb were quietly trying to picture a moon-resurrecting faith. The idea surpassed anything ordinary; a fantasy of extraordinary mind bending.

While they were thinking, the Hunter walked up, chuckled and said, "It takes the vision of a goat for my sheep to see the obvious." Jesus put his arms around their shoulders and chided,

"Quit trying to figure it out and believe. It's so simple."

"I can *picture* it happening, Jesus," Bobby stated. "I think it can be done. — No, I *know* it can be done. But believing that it *will* be done — that's a big simple."

"There's a thin line between thinking and faithing; knowing and believing. You can know my word well and still not believe it. Positionally, it's like walking through a membrane or veil. All you have to do is step through that veil and what you could only see before is now possible."

"How do I get through that veil?" Caleb asked.

"If you live in life-union with me and if my words live power-fully within you—then you can ask whatever you desire and it will be done. When your life bears that kind of abundant fruit, you prove that you are my mature disciples who glorify my Father."[5]

Caleb's face screwed up with incomprehension. "You mean I can ask for anything I want, and it will be done?"

"I tell you this timeless truth, Caleb: The person who follows me in faith, believing in me, will do the same mighty miracles that I did—and even greater miracles than those I did when I was here because I went to my Father after my crucifixion! I will do whatever you ask me to do when you ask in my name."[6]

"So, it's not about what I want; it's something more?" Caleb responded.

"I have commissioned you, as sons of God, to go into the world to bear fruit. And your fruit will last, because whatever you ask of my father, *for my sake,* he will give it to you!"[7]

"I see it. We don't ask for greedy desires to be done. We ask for kingdom desires to be done."

"Everything I did then on earth; and still do now; was and is motivated by love. Your greatest asset and power is faith motivated by love. Faith motivated by love will change the world. So be careful to examine your motives to make sure your life is filled with love when you do your good deeds."[8]

"I can see that I don't see as well as I need to see." Bobby concluded with a sigh.

Jesus took him by the shoulders and smiled. "Don't give up. Every persistent person will get what he asks for. Every persistent seeker will discover what he needs. And everyone who persistently knocks will find an open door."[9] He looked at their uncertain faces and added, "And with that, I will let the three of you have some time to consider what you're going to do about this problem."

Scampy started laughing; which sounded like hysterical bleating. Bobby put his hands in his pockets, shook his head and smiled. Caleb looked around and exclaimed, "Wait a minute." But the Hunter was gone. "I Could have used more input."

Scampy's laughter slowed to a chuckle. "I love these adventures. They are what make up the stories of our tribe. It will be an honor to be a part of this one."

"Scampy," Bobby said. "Come to Mama Rachel's house. We'll grab some lawn chairs and make ourselves comfortable. I could use a blanket to help me get warm. — Guys, we've been handed our solution. It could take hours, days or weeks to wrap our faith around this and unpack a plan."

Scampy broke into laughter again but didn't say why.

Caleb wondered about Scampy's worldview. With a twisted smile, he thought it would be awkward to ask. He was confident it was nothing like his own. Instead, he asked Bobby, "Do you have any idea where to begin?"

"Yes, I do. We need to talk about our experience. It will give us an idea of how to develop an action plan. . . Scampy, talk to me about your flock."

"From the days of my great grandfather and the other patriarchs, we have experienced great healings, resurrections and amazing visitations. There are stories upon stories from then until now of prayers that have helped us. In our tribe, miracles are normal."

As they approached the house, Rachel's cats ran up to Scampy. "Hi friends," Scampy greeted as they mewed and rubbed his legs. He listened a moment and stated, "My name is Scampy, who are you?" He listened as they responded.

"You understand them?" Caleb asked.

"Yes, this too is normal."

Caleb was fascinated. He reacted with, "Why don't we go find Scampy's goat tribe, and have *them* pray for a brand-new moon?"

"That's not the assignment we were given," Bobby responded firmly. "He said *we* were to solve the problem."

"If Scampy has the faith to pray for a new moon," Caleb reasoned, "he should pray and we'll pray along with him."

"It doesn't work that way, Caleb. Jesus says: 'I give you an eternal truth: If two of you agree to ask God for something in a symphony of prayer, my heavenly Father will do it for you. For wherever two or three come together in honor of my name, I am right there with them!'[10] We can't just sing the same song Scampy's singing and not have the faith he's believing with."

"You won't like the way I sing," Scampy rejoined.

'That's a metaphor, Scampy" Bobby said with a chuckle. "The sound is not important when the song; or prayer; is in agreement with heaven. It's about the harmony and unison of our hearts honoring the heart of Jesus. So Scampy, tell us how you guys are so powerful when you pray."

Scampy thought while staring at the bushes. He turned to Bobby and said, "I don't know. We've been doing it for generations. It's just normal. Praying for a new moon wouldn't be any different than praying for a broken hoof. It should simply happen. But I can't explain it."

"Great!" Caleb exclaimed saucily. "If we don't know how . . . then . . . *how?*

"Having knowledge," Bobby responded, "or knowing how, is not what we're looking for. We aren't going to think about a new moon, know how to create it and *poof,* there it is. We need spiritual power; the same power Joshua had when he spoke to the sun and moon to stand still."[11]

"You mean," Caleb interjected, "when the *earth* stood still."

"Yes Caleb," Bobby said with a huff. "I'm simply quoting what they understood in their day."

"You guys are making my head stand still," Scampy stated, shaking his horns.

"Listen Bobby, doesn't that story say there was no day like it before or since that God heeded the voice of a man? Who are we?"

"We are not mere men. We are God's sons with a destiny to be as big as Jesus is.[12] And by living in Christ, love has been brought to its full expression in us. All that Jesus now is, so are we in this world.[13] He's seated at the right hand of the Father *in the Heavenly realm,* and so are we."[14]

"You have some tasty grass here, Bobby," Scampy stated. "I like it better than the meadow grass."

"You're welcome to join the conversation, Scampy," Caleb said sarcastically.

"No need," Scampy responded undeterred. "I'll let you people work on it."

"We could use your help."

"Okay . . ." Scampy thought a few seconds. "What Jesus said should settle it. How long would this talk last if you actually *believed* what he said?"

"So, what you're saying," Bobby interjected, "is that we aren't going to increase our faith or believe more perfectly by talking about it."

Scampy shook his ears. "I don't get what Jesus meant by a veil; I don't know what that is. But in the flock, we have a thing we call crossing the chicken line. We encourage the young goats to picture it in their imagination as they learn to pray for miracles. Could it be something like that?

"Of course, the young ones see the older ones do miracles all the time. So that makes it easier to *show* them faith rather than talk about it."

"Finding the golden scroll was the first of several miracles," Caleb stated. "Although it encourages me to believe that miracles happen, it hasn't given me a moon-forming faith. That idea doesn't seem to be gelling. Getting through this veil or crossing the chicken line, as you call it, looks more like a great leap. Something needs to be revealed."

"Let's take a walk," Bobby stated. "I always think better when I'm moving."

"There's that pathway up to the rock, Bobby," Scampy exclaimed. "Do you remember it?"

"Yeah, Scampy. My dad and I had some great adventures up there. Grandma Rachel told me about my great-grandfather having visions on that rock. It has a great view of the valley and a history of spiritual experiences . . . How about if you lead the way."

"Keep up if you can." Scampy laughed as he bounded ahead.

Bobby rejoined with a chuckle, "I know the way, you ornery horn-head. See you there."

The hike took them through the meadowed neighborhood and into a grove of trees where the evening twilight barely revealed leafy ground in the shadows. A well-worn pathway from years of hoof and boot lay before them.

"This must be a popular destination," Caleb said.

"If I remember rightly," Bobby responded, "there's a steep climb up ahead. It'll be good exercise for us and get our blood circulating."

By the time Bobby and Caleb reached the top of the path at the rear of the rock outcrop, they were winded and energized at the same time. And light was fading.

At the front of the ledge, Scampy stood next to a woman. They were looking out over the valley. The woman was rubbing Scampy behind his ears and humming a tune. Her form was the trim physique of someone who took care of herself and approached five and a half feet tall. She wore a wide-brimmed hat and knitted sweater.

"Hi Grandma," Bobby said affectionately and gave her a hug. "I should have expected you to be here."

"My father came here every morning to watch the sun rise and pray. He said that God's voice was in the sunrise and sunset each day. Since my return to Wonder Valley, I have endeavored to follow in his steps. Jesus told me that this land is deeply vested with the presence of God, and began generations before my father's time. It's a very special place to the Lord.

"I have seen and heard great things from this rock, just as my father did. The destiny of nations has been determined by intercession from this rock. Your father had a different calling, and therefore had no drawing to come here. But what your great-grandfather and I have had, is now extended to you as a legacy."

She placed her hands on Bobby's head, then moved one hand to Caleb and another to Scampy and prayed, "Be blessed with the honor of sitting at the feet of Jesus."

She stood back and added, "I understand you three have been given an urgent mission and I am not to interfere in any way." She acknowledged it sadly and finished with a sigh of contentment, "And with that, I will leave you to it."

"Grandma, you could be so helpful to us. Your experience . . ."

She held up a hand to interrupt. "I am not to interfere, Bobby. Jesus knows why and he knows what he's doing. Trust him and him alone.

"Now I must go before I say too much." She smiled again, then turned and headed for the trail. A trio of squirrels raced up to her along the way. She laughed as if they were small children wanting her attention and conversed with them as she walked. The guys could hear the chatter between them, but couldn't understand what was said.

"This is indeed a valley of wonder," Caleb stated.

Scampy chuckled. "You have no idea, Caleb. You must stay for a while and hear the stories. Our historian has the skill to remember everything passed to him from the legendary Tanny. He was the master storyteller from the ancient times. I never tire of hearing of Papa God's choosing of this valley and what he did during the days of Mama and Papa Shepherd when the goat herd visited heaven and began to talk."

"Didn't I just hear the squirrels talking?" Caleb asked.

"That's normal, Caleb" Bobby responded.

"That also began in those days," Scampy added. "We call it The Ruction, a time of supernatural change."

They stood looking down on the valley a few minutes; man and beast gathering their thoughts.

Bobby turned around to search the forest and spotted what appeared to be an interwoven archway made of two gnarled oak trees. It sparked the idea of a portal. The words "ancient times" returned from something Scampy said.

"Guys, I think we need to hear those ancient stories," Bobby said calmly.

"That's exactly what I was thinking," Caleb rejoined.

"Me too," added Scampy.

"How do we get there, Scampy?" Bobby asked.

"We go through those two trees and into the forest. It's not far beyond that."

"We'll start after breakfast in the morning," Bobby responded.

Chapter Thirty-two

The cool morning air was alternately piney then musty; a result of the presence of old digger pines and decades of oak leaves falling in their season. A composting blanket of mulch made for soft yet slow walking. Occasional meadows provided green for the eyes and grazing for deer. The oak groves were nearly cold in the shade, their leaves completing their change to autumn colors. The weak diggers had cast down wind-broken limbs to make their hike a greater effort with walking around or going over.

"I thought you said it wasn't far," Caleb whined. "We've gone at least three miles, maybe four."

"What's a mile?" Scampy responded.

"Caleb," Bobby injected. "Animals aren't concerned with time and distance. It's an altogether different paradigm for them."

"It took me less time to get to you," Scampy declared, "than it has to return."

"Why is that, Scampy?" Caleb asked.

"Uhhh, I asked an angel to carry me. There was no time involved at all."

Caleb raised his hands; bothered, "Well, that makes sense. Why didn't we think of that?"

"I didn't see any angels," Scampy responded simply.

Caleb stuffed his tired annoyance, sighed and groaned, "I'm

getting really thirsty.”

“You’ll love the water where we live. It’s quite sweet and very cold.” Scampy chuckled and added, “And I’ve heard stories of what it does to the people who drink it. Spooky stuff.”

“Anybody ever tell you,” Bobby chimed in laughing, “that you have a mischievous streak in you?”

“I don’t know what mis . chiff . us means.”

“Rascal, prankster, practical joker; that kind of stuff.”

Scampy laughed. “Oh that! Yeah, it runs in my family. That’s why I was named after my great grandfather. I’ve been told that I’m just like him.”

“Hey look!” Caleb exclaimed. “There’s an old cabin up ahead.”

“We’re almost there,” Scampy stated.

As they approached the cabin Caleb added, “I hear a creek or something; water’s nearby.”

When they were past the dilapidated cabin, the guys caught a glimpse of the water source. Beyond the undergrowth, a serene picture opened up. A stone outcrop about ten feet high formed a grotto over a pond and extended to the right to create a natural rise and wall. Water lazily poured over the stone ledge and into the pond.

Caleb saw a flat area that gave access to the pond and headed for it. He got on his knees and using his hand for a cup, drank slowly. Then laying flat, he stuck his lips in the water and pulled deeply. He jerked and yelled, “Brain freeze! Careful Bobby, this stuff is ice cold. But it’s so sweet, I don’t want to stop.”

Bobby stood gazing into the water with scientific eyes and marveled, “How strange, the water has a purple hue to it. It has to be fed by a natural spring from a source deep enough to tap rare minerals. And judging by the bubble-like formation of the ponding area, there's volcanic solids dissolved in there, too." He smiled and added, "This stuff might actually be good for you."

He bent and drank cautiously, then drank some more.

Scampy drank as well, then said flatly, "I heard a story of a man that had visions because of the water here; traveled through time, it is said." He let the statement soak in while watching the faces of Bobby and Caleb look at each other wondering. — When the timing was right, he laughed heartily. "The flock is up on the higher ground where there's more grass and leafy plants."

"I really need to dial up my sense of humor, Bobby." Caleb groaned.

Bobby chuckled. "We might just learn to laugh again, Caleb. There is something about this place. I'm thinking differently already . . . maybe it *is* the water. . . Scampy, once again, lead the way."

Their journey around and up took them to an open patch of meadowland where goats of all sizes and colors grazed, loafed and played. But when the humans arrived, all came running; curious about their visitors.

Scampy made introductions with little regard for the human inability to remember everyone. He knew them all, and they all wanted to know everything about these humans. Questions grew to a ruckus then declined. When Scampy told the goat herd that Bobby was Rachels grandson, an awe descended on the group.

Scampy gave the reason for Bobby and Caleb's visit. Its significance was not lost with the goats. Wanting to know the old stories had a lot of significance. The got flock's legacy reminded them of their promises of a powerful future. Heads turned to an older goat who was smiling broadly.

"This is Oracle," Scampy said. "He is the only living son of Tanny, the great historian who lived during the time of the Ruction. The flock lived in the valley at the time. The Hunter moved everyone here after the valley increased in people. And Oracle has been passing on the history of our tribe to two of his sons, who will take his place."

"Your visit is very timely, my friends," Oracle stated slowly. "I have been very fortunate to live longer than any of my generation. But I know that my time of departure is coming, and I'm looking forward to seeing my loved ones again.

"But I was told by the Hunter of souls, that I would tell these precious stories one more time to humans before I go. Have you met the Hunter? Do you possess his great favor and love?"

"Yes to both questions, Oracle," Bobby answered. Oracle's demeanor was royal; even reverent. Bobby spoke to him accordingly. "I consider it an honor to be in his presence at all times, and a privilege to have the opportunity to hear the testimonies of this tribe and their encounters with the mighty Hunter."

"That is good, young one. You would not understand these stories unless you possessed the great one's love. They would be foolishness to you.

"Please make yourself comfortable and I will begin when you are ready . . . But first, let us regather near the spring that feeds the waterhole below us. Being near it refreshment will help me to speak and it will help you to listen."

When Oracle began his narrative, all weariness of age vanished. His voice cleared and an anointing filled the atmosphere. For three days, he told histories and testimonies stored up in his spirit. There were valuable lessons of life, heroic adventures, supernatural encounters and a peculiar story of a deadly enemy who became a friend.

The time sped by. Listening was not wearying nor uncomfortable. Oracle's words were magnetic and alive. One could picture his stories easily and feel a part of those times and seasons. Although the flock had heard these stories before, they gladly heard them again.

At sunset, the kids were taken care of and a pause was given until sunrise for the little ones to rest. Bobby and Caleb slept with the flock to keep warm. Being without food didn't matter; the stories were like food that satisfied.

By mid-afternoon of the third day, Oracle finished with all that was in him. "There is more, but they are mere reports of events. They are not important to what I have been told to give you . . . Now if you will excuse me, I need a nap. It has been a treasure to be your humble servant. Good day and good life to you, my friends."

Bobby rose from his cross-legged position and laid hands on the horns of the old Oracle. "May your final days be filled with the joyous expectation of a great reward. Well done good and faithful servant."

Bobby stepped back and said respectfully, "Thank you, Oracle. I will never forget this visit. I have indeed been made rich by it."

"Indeed you have, and so have I. Good bye, my friends. I will see you again after I am made younger through my passing."

"I'm ready to go whenever you are," Caleb said. "I am seriously hungry. It would be nice to get back."

Bobby nodded his head and stated, "Well Scampy, let's get going. We have a moon to restore."

"Head for the cabin," Scampy responded. "The path is just beyond it."

As they approached the crumbling cabin, Caleb stopped and asked with hopeful eyes, "Can we take a look inside before we go?" And then with peevish look added, "Who knows what treasure lurks behind yonder door for us to discover?"

"I'm game," Bobby replied with a grin that suggested fun.

Scampy followed them adding the flat comment, "I've seen it before."

What was left of the partially open door fell unexpectedly as Caleb pressed against it. The crash sent bugs and dust scurrying. The door cracked when Caleb stepped on it. "Where there's bugs, there's spiders," Caleb said remembering a lesson from his dad's wilderness instructions. "Watch yourself."

Once inside, there was little to get excited about. A worn and grainy wood sign hung over the rock hearth, its shadow of writing unreadable. Animal traps crusted with corrosion hung nearby, the remains of a bird's nest cradled within it. The cabin's roof was somewhere in the composted mulch of the floor. Caleb was about to recommend leaving. It wasn't safe.

"What's that?" Bobby asked.

A rumble had started in the floor, sending vibrations up their legs. Unexpectedly, the wall opposite the door fell, raising more dust. From the middle of the cloud a shimmering opaque window appeared. It grew from the size of a postcard and filled the opening. Once formed, it became crystal clear, revealing a tunnel of branches with golden autumn leaves. At the end was the arched portal of oak trees; brilliant light shining on the other side of its opening.

"I told you," stated Scampy with an excited chuckle and added a kid-goat prance to go with it. "There's something in the water."

They carefully waded through the debris on the floor, then through the wall and into the tunnel. After clearing the fallen wall, the loud slam of a door closing came from behind them. They turned to see the log wall back in place.

From where they stood to the other side of the oaken arch was the distance of a football field. It was an easy walk to the arch. And as they stood under it, the rock outcrop invited them to the ledge lit by afternoon sun.

As Bobby looked down from the ledge at the various estates that peppered the scene, his attention was captured by the observatory his father built for him when he was a preteen.

The beginning and the end, he thought to himself. Maybe it wasn't his own thoughts, though; sometimes it was hard to tell his own heart from Holy Spirit's. He wasn't sure what it meant. He squinted his eyes and wondered once more. This journey began with a telescope on a barren mountain in South America more than seventeen years ago. Maybe this will end with one in a quiet valley of where wonders are normal.

Chapter Thirty-three

A press release from Bobby, given that afternoon, informed the global public that a solution for the earth's gravitational dilemma would be revealed by morning. He gave it remotely so he wouldn't have to face the grilling of contentious questions a live press conference often delivered.

The sun had set and it was a perfect time to observe the night sky.

The dome for Bobby's sixteen-inch star-finder telescope sat on a ten-foot high cinderblock room surrounded with green hedging. Inside, stairs provided access to the dome. A mere ten feet in diameter, it was tight for two people and a goat. Their immediate purpose was to get a look at the debris field created by the impact of asteroid and moon.

Bobby glanced at the four-inch screen on his wrist to verify astral coordinates. It interfaced with his telescope's computer. "That should do it," he said and tapped the screen. The high whine of the reduction motor cut through the still night as it rotated the turret of the dome. Bobby turned on the monitor and waited for the telescope's objective to appear.

"It looks like a dust cloud in my dad's shop," Caleb stated. "There aren't any big chunks."

"After all this time," Bobby responded, "those big *chunks* are thirty million miles beyond the smaller particles. I'll have to increase magnification to find those chunks. But that isn't the point at this time."

"My guess is," Caleb stated, "you're pushing us forward and giving us a direction to focus on."

"That's right. No turning back and no back door," Bobby responded. "We've crossed the chicken line."

Scampy thought for a moment. "I'm ready." He shook his head and let it continue to his tail. "I have a good feeling about this. What do we do next?"

Bobby smiled and stated, "Jesus told us that 'your life will be fruitless unless you live your life intimately joined to mine.'[1] Let's get connected with him."

"Remember the words the Hunter gave us when we were at Grandma Rachel's house?" Caleb asked. "If you live in life-union with me and if my words live powerfully within you—then you can ask whatever you desire and it will be done."[2]

"Yeah," Bobby responded. "That's a good reminder."

"We should sing something from that," Scampy stated expectantly.

"Sing it?" Caleb rejoined. "Sing scripture?"

"Good idea, Scampy." Bobby exclaimed. "It'll give us a frequency to align with heaven."

"What's a frequency?" Scampy asked.

"What I'm talking about is a quantum physics theory that everything in the universe; including creation; has its own wave length on earth and in heaven. If we join those creative wave sounds in perfect alignment, anything can happen."

"Oh." Scampy thought briefly then added, "Do goats need to know that?"

"Your faith is beyond all that, Scampy. You're good just the way you are. But for a guy like me, it's important."

Bobby tapped the screen on his wrist and started background music through the speakers. Scampy hummed at first, then began a little two-step dance. Caleb joined in creating more human-like dance steps. Bobby appeared self-conscious at first, but threw it off and jumped in.

Caleb sang, declaring the heart of heaven.

"The Hunter has declared it, it's his will to cure the moon.
Heaven has aligned with him to see it done real soon.
And we agree, Jesus, we exalt your name.
And we agree, Jesus, what we do is for your fame.
You're the one, who sang and made the universe.
We're the ones, who call back what has been dispersed,
Yes we call, come back.
We proclaim, come back.
Let all decree, come back.
Heaven calls, come back."

Scampy picked up the prophetic minstrelizing as a shift in the spiritual atmosphere moved away from natural.

"I'm calling you, I'm calling you,
all you pieces of the moon.
Hear my voice, hear my voice,
all the world will rejoice.
Come from rock, come from dust,
Come from nothing if you must.
Make more light, make moon light,
Don't resist our source of might.

Moon stop your run to the blackhole,
Reaching out with a big o lasso,
We capture moonbeams in our loophole,
And call you back, and call you back.
Outside of time, inside the fun,
Come back before the rising sun."

Bobby slid the music volume up then yelled, "Everybody sing 'come back.'" The three sang swelling choruses of "Come back" over and over.

The monitor turned to blue screen then returned to the picture of space that was previously there. The words "come back" appeared embossed on the screen and floated into space. As soon as one faded into the distance another appeared and followed it; repeating itself as they sang.

A low hum joined them and filled everything. It fluctuated from nearly too loud to soft and then higher in pitch to lower.

The dome wall shimmered, shifted to translucent with shadows beyond, then shuttered transparent. The night outside was illuminated by their light from within; the shrubbery could be seen. The roof of the dome peeled back, the cinderblock wall snaked past it and headed for space, funneling as it went, until it twisted and spun out of sight. Colors beyond earthly norms appeared like swirls over the face of the wall.

A broad highland with pastures appeared on the walls; a scene from another world. Unusual trees appeared; hundreds of feet tall that sprouted from its ground. The leaves of the trees formed and gave off music as they grew. Their tones resonated beyond the natural ear and back again, yet affected beautiful harmonies.

"The leaves are singing the names of God," Bobby declared loudly to overcome the increased volume. He hesitated between statements. "I hear the song with my body . . . violin strings are being played inside me . . . Creation is being released through the funnel."

Distance out through the funnel lost its earthly perception and time was captured in its influence. They could see close and far at the same time.

"I wanna help!" Caleb yelled not knowing what he was saying. "Woohoo!" By simply thinking it, he was suddenly gone and postured behind an enormous clod of moon. He stopped its flight with little effort. "Go back and be made new," he told it.

The hunk dissolved, reshaped itself like a long, thin balloon and sped back toward earth without hesitation.

"Come on, guys. Help me out."

Bobby and Scampy were there in a heartbeat. Scampy used his horns to redirect a chunk a hundred times his size. He looked like a tugboat altering the course of an ocean liner. Bobby shot smaller pieces like basketballs through hoops that swished into the chain of moon pieces returning by way of the walls of the funnel. The leaves and limbs of the trees bucket brigaded pieces back toward their place.

Laughter exploded from everywhere. The Hunter arrived on a horse made of moon dust. He laughed hilariously and spurred his ride like a rodeo cowboy.

"Great idea, guys" Jesus yelled. "The herd is following behind." A cloud of moon rocks followed him making cattle sounds.

Caleb quickly shaped a similar horse and handed it off to Bobby. Bobby climbed on, yelled "Gitup" and off he galloped. Caleb looked at Scampy wondering what he should create for him.

Scampy said, "I'm good," and scampered away. Caleb fashioned a large horse for himself and rode to the back of the flow to spur things on.

The enormous vortex of the funnel chorused sounds of winds that whistled at differing speeds. As men, moon and messiah drew back, the funnel collapsed, warped or otherwise retreated. The scene was beyond words to describe as the walls morphed from transparent to obscure.

Without time, it was hard to determine how long. But everyone was back inside the observatory. The walls and dome were normal. Now there were four in the room and huddled close.

On the monitor was a moon in stunning brilliance against a backdrop of deep space.

"Woohoo," Caleb yelled. "Let's go outside and look at this thing!"

Excited, the troop burst down the stairs and out the door and took up a clear-sighted position in the yard. The sky was azure in the dawn's twilight; a full night had passed; and the moon gleamed brilliantly in its fulness. A seeming white cue ball glowed before them; a moon without the wounds of ancient craters from space objects striking it to break up its surface.

Jesus jested with Caleb. "I understand you were caught up in the emotion of the moment. But next time you should declare a vintage moon instead of a brand new one."

"Wow, it is bright, isn't it?" Caleb responded.

"Fresh off the showroom floor," Bobby announced. "Didn't the other one have mountains?"

"Hills, yes," Jesus stated with a chuckle. "Mountains, not so much. — "But, no worries, I'll get my angels working on it. A little pressure here and some distressing there, they'll have fun making it look like an old new moon."

"Now I see," Bobby stated, "how all the craters and ridges tempered the moon's brilliance. It's overwhelming without them. It's more than amazing to see it back in place."

As levity and adrenalin subsided, awe quietly filled their emotions. They had witnessed creation alongside the creator and the resumption of time that had slipped out and back to an eternal world while they were gone.

"This will make a story the flock will talk about for a long time," Scampy mused. "I wonder how it looked from where they are? How do I describe to them what we just did?"

Jesus knew their thoughts. "You're right. There are no earthly words to describe what you experienced. You would have to be in heaven to even apprehend it. And yet, it is written that you are seated with me in those heavenly places. Things never discovered or heard of before, things beyond your ability to imagine — these are the many things God has in store for all his lovers.[3] And now, you have expressed it for me."

Jesus extended his arms and hugged each one tenderly. When Bobby hugged the Hunter he added, "You're such an amazing friend to let us be a part of this. Thank you."

"You guys are the amazing ones," Jesus responded. "You heard my word and agreed with it. You loved me and obeyed my directive to heal this planet. And for my sake, you asked of my Father for this great miracle; such a miracle that has not been done since we spoke this universe into being. You are indeed, my disciples."

Jesus turned to Bobby and Caleb with anticipation in his eyes. "And now, I commission the two of you to go and proclaim my good news of salvation while the world has your attention. Tell them how much I love them. Tell them of the sacrifice I made to remove their sins. And show them my love by healing their bodies and hearts and raising their dead.

"And when you have finished testifying of me, the world will rise up and kill you."

"You're kidding, aren't you?" Caleb asked in shock. "After what we did?"

"You have seen it already, Caleb. The world has hated you without a cause. You had nothing to do with the calamity that destroyed the moon. Yet the world hated you and wanted to kill you. Just because the moon is back in its place, nothing has changed. Yes, many will believe. And sadly, many will continue to harden their hearts and not turn to me.

"Remember Lazarus? I raised him from the grave with an

indisputable miracle in Israel. Many of the Jews believed in me because of it. And many others determined from that day forward to not only kill me, but Lazarus also.

"This miracle of a restored moon is also indisputable throughout the world. Yet the results will be no different.

"The world hates you because it first hated me. If you were to give your allegiance to the world, they would love and welcome you as one of their own. But because you won't align yourself with their values, they will hate you.[4]

"But I have called you as witnesses of me. You belong to me, and I will protect you until the time comes when my purposes with you are finished. Then you will be welcomed in my Father's house and receive the reward of your labors and sacrifices of love for me."

"What about me, Papa Shepherd?" Scampy asked. "Can I go home now?"

"Yes, my friend. Your tribe has never said no to me; always faithful. The flock has known the legacy of my presence for many generations, Scampy. That will continue in hiddenness until the end. I will call upon your family again when I have need.

"Thank you for your service, Scampy. Return to the flock and rest. This is certainly one of the flock's best stories."

Scampy nodded his head reverently and said, "It has been my honor to serve you, Jesus, and be the voice of a story that will certainly honor you. I'm excited to go back and tell it."

"We could not have done this without you, Scampy." Bobby inserted. "The inspiration of your faith and the testimonies of your tribe are priceless gems, gold and silver in our Father's Kingdom. If I don't see you again in this life, I will see you and all your namesake in the life to come. It has been my honor that our families have been reunited to change the world around us once again."[5]

"I will be on my way" responded Scampy expectantly. "I bid you all good day and blessed life."

Jesus rubbed him behind the ears, then knelt and hugged him around the neck. When Jesus stood, Scampy bolted off, kicking up his heels like a kid. "Oh, did we have *fun!*" was heard in the distance.

Jesus chuckled, then turned to Bobby and Caleb. "It is time for you to appear before the cameras and give your proof of me. There are selfish interests already scheming to take credit for what has happened. They will attempt to deceive the people and turn their hearts away from me.

"You must tell the truth and oppose them for my sake. You have saved the moon. But only my love will save the world. Have no fear, be bold and courageous. I will be with you."

PART 2

FIRESIDE CHATS

Conversations at Oxford

Introduction with Caleb

What you just read about the restoring of the moon has had no equal since then. It was a magnificent adventure and certainly not the last of other challenges. Frankly, Bobby and I are amazed we have lived this long. Through it all we have learned to see with our spirit, not with our eyes. It was a unique education.

My time at Oxford wasn't all adventure and hard knocks. Bobby, Professor Sholom, Sherlock Holmes and even Doctor Watson were there in the thick of my circumstances to impart practical lessons along with emotional and spiritual wisdom. Sometimes, the impartations came through a British stiff upper lip; straight up and direct. At other times, Bobby's brotherly chats and comic relief got me on track when I felt jaded or wanted to feel sorry for myself. Even today, fun-loving banter between us often leads to enlightenment.

So, what I gained wasn't exclusive of the golden scroll experience. The relationships that started there added richness. And our talks were extra nuggets mined for a more complete treasure of immeasurable wealth.

When I returned home, I was compelled to diligently journal everything before fine details faded. Because I did, you got to read my story. And now, you get to learn how to unlock the golden scroll for yourself.

During the years since then, I started revising journal entries with mature language and clearer narrative. I stopped when I realized my entries were losing their youth.

So, I passed my journals on to the author of this book. He transcribed them and said he would make something from it all. I thought he meant that he would clean up the grammar and organize the content; nothing serious.

When I received a manuscript from him for my approval, I was surprised. He captured something powerful that I had not seen. He wrote to hearts that could gain what I gained. Bobby and have I approved the project and now, it moves forward.

From his generosity, you can extract nuggets of life from the golden scroll of God's Word through tools presented in this second part. So, I dedicate these tools for your use. Through them, may you increase in your worship of God in Spirit and in truth, and gain understanding of spiritual realities.

I will look forward to hearing about your progress.

Author's note to readers

Before this book was finished, Bobby and Caleb were martyred. Their message was and will always be polarizing. It's hard to comprehend how God's love for us through his son Jesus can provoke such ferocious response. But their passion *required* a response, and their message *demands* one to choose life or death. New life is ignited with the acceptance of it, with an abundant life sustained in the flames of living it through faith.

Bobby and Caleb were reformers and advancers of the Kingdom of God to the core. They knew the cost and never backed down; it was their baptism of fire. None of their words went unsupported by heaven. Even their end was glorious. When they were killed, their bodies were left in the streets to rot. I get goosebumps remembering what happened next.

With the entire planet looking on by satellite, they came back to life after three days. Like triumphant conquerors, they raised their faces and hands toward heaven in praise. And in that instant, they were lifted from this planet as the loud blast of a trumpet sounded.

That event triggered ripples throughout the earth. Their message was the Son of Man who overcame the power of this world by his crucifixion on a cross. Multitudes turned their hearts and believed he is the Son of God who rose from the dead. The God of all gods released a time of revival and transformation in every place where two or three gathered. No words are grand enough to describe that season in our lives. The living Word and Spirit had more life and reality than at any time in church history. What took place was beyond anything we could imagine.

And so, I am privileged to tell their story. My years spent with them help me to share that story and these conversations with the strong conviction that it is all for your benefit. Along with Caleb, it is my hope you will find these conversations meaningful, humorous and productive.

I would be unrealistic to think every tool in this crib will find a home in your heart. If only one or two are activated, I will have honored the memories of those who have affected my life so deeply. Diligence to these will kindle a blazing story in your life.

Bobby and Caleb were fathers of the faith in every sense. They had families and other spiritual children that continue their legacy. Their families want you to run the race as Bobby and Caleb did. If you follow them as they followed the Hunter, you will leave a heritage also.

It is comforting that our message continues through Jesus' disciples; including our wives and our children. The never-ending good news progresses from generation to generation to give birth to the Children of God.

After all has been said, *Unlocking the Golden Scroll* is more than a story. It's a search for incalculable wealth in the secret and mysterious places where Father God is found. He is findable . . . when you look for him with all your heart.

And there are those unexpected moments when he finds us. He is the Hunter, you know.

Peeling the Layers

When Professor Sholom brought up getting together to go over his approach to studying the Bible, I responded with the suggested that the idea sounded dull and boring. He understood how a youth of my age would come to that conclusion, then corrected me and got to "the heart of the matter," as he put it. Alluding to the golden scroll and the considerable worth of it and the Word of God as described in Psalm 119:162 as being treasure, he threw out the phrase unlocking the golden scroll as an alternative way for me to view this discipline. Study tools were the keys for unlocking the revelational mysteries and spiritual realities in the Word that becomes the riches and power of the Kingdom of God.

I liked the feel of it. From then on, it worked for me.

Today, after years into this adventure, I have discovered there are more treasures than ever to be unlocked in the golden scroll. That truth makes me a passionate treasure hunter, because I know beyond any doubt that I could never exhaust the supply of brilliant revelation hidden in it. Along with that gold is the interactive connection that allows God to unlock my heart for the transformational gold he works within. Back to the point.

My first meeting with Professor Sholom about this was to hear his ideas about what he would teach me as keys for unlocking the golden scroll. I came to his office after his morning lecture. He was hyper, as he always seemed to be. I figured out that he came alive when people shared their thoughts in response to what he had to say. He was even more energetic that day, having had an exhilarating row (British term for disagreement) with one of his students.

"Top of the morning to you, Caleb. Come in and have a seat . .

. Ah, but first, could you make some tea?"

"Sure Professor. It would be my pleasure." I had learned well from Bobby.

"You have done well learning the way I like it. Someday you'll make a surpassing Englishman."

"I can't wait to hang that certificate on my wall." He knew I was referring to the assorted diplomas of earned and honored degrees on the walls of his office. After returning to the states, I was honored to receive such a certificate from the school. It is proudly displayed in my home.

The professor laughed and said, "Good show, you're catching the drift of it."

After I made tea, we sat down and I listened.

"When I was a boy, Caleb, I remember word-for-word a children's movie that was old even then. You may never have heard of it. It left an indelible impression on the way I approach learning. I call it the layer principle, and the movie scene went a bit like this:

"Shrek the ogre and Donkey, who just happened to be a donkey, are having a conversation. 'There's a lot more to ogres than people think,' Shrek tells Donkey. "Ogres are like onions. Onions have layers. Ogres have layers."

"Donkey, in response, takes a whiff of the half-eaten onion that Shrek just threw down and says quaintly, 'Ya know, not everybody like onions.' Then, with an epiphonal declaration he yells, "Cakes! Everybody loves cakes. Cakes have layers, too."

"For Shrek, further expansion or exchange on the premise was unacceptable. Onions were the simile of the day; end of story. Just peel back the layers and you'll discover the makeup of the ogre. And yet, the layers are the ogre.

194

"Here's my point, Caleb. For us English Bible readers our layer peeling experience starts with some nine hundred translations, paraphrases, revisions and corrections that have been written since 1576.[1] Finding them in hard copy would intimidate even the most adventurous soul and cost a fortune. Reading all of them to gain their particular insights would take an enormous amount of time.

"What I propose is, forget about the layers and just become the onion. But, to become the onion one must learn to integrate particular layers."

"Professor, I think I'm a little confused," I confessed.

"That's because you're viewing the onion as a whole. It's too complex. To simplify, you learn the layers and put the smaller pieces together for a brand-new whole.

"Can you put that in plain English?" I asked.

"Indeed. Become the Word of God by taking it apart and putting it back together. You study to take it apart and understand the layers. Then rebuild the layers from the inside out to become the whole from within.

"Paul says to let the word of Christ live in you richly, flooding you with all wisdom.[2] What better way to become the word than by putting it in you one layer at a time?"

I struggled with his concept. It was simply too . . . organic or something; I could see it, but then again not clearly. It wasn't until I got through other lessons that it began to take shape. And because I grew up building things with my dad, I ditched the layer principle and replaced it with building language. Foundations, walls, roofs, water and other functional utilities were parts I understood. I grasped from then on, that the idea is to take the large parts and dismantle them until I see the small parts. When I see them clearly, I put them back together as bigger and bigger parts until I could make a whole part. What I understand now is, whether I use the layers or parts simile, I can peel back the Word and put it back together in a variety of ways and retain the same message.

What I'm not saying is that I can put it back together any way I please. What I am saying is that I can create smaller or bigger pictures that give me resources from which to draw useful illustrations of life that apply to given contexts. I have practiced moving and restructuring the parts with verified accuracy so I can impart life to those who hear me. Now, it comes to me naturally during a conversation and I enjoy seeing the ah ha expressions on the participant's face as they grasp the illustrations.

The Defining Factors

Bobby and I were having a great time of basketball at the professor's house one afternoon. When I say great, it means I was winning. Our fun was followed by a spontaneous lesson about definitions.

Bobby threw out a bible verse that had been on his mind, "Scripture says that God conceals the revelation of what he is saying in the hiding place of his glory. But the honor of kings is revealed by how they thoroughly investigate the deeper message of all that God says."[1]

I attempted to draw a conclusion. "What you're saying is, if we find out what that deeper message is, then we'll know why we're here?" It turned out I wasn't seeing the bigger picture.

"Caleb, two things are obvious. One, you *have* been given a message. The second thing is, we were put together right after it came. That leaves us some potential conclusions. I believe we are meant to work together with a combined and larger message. And, that we are to help each other discover more about our message and get an idea of what to do with it."

"It sounds like a story that washed ashore in a bottle," I said. "My message came in a cylinder from space written in an ancient language. Yours is coming in an asteroid with *unknown* written all over it." I had to give that backdrop some verbal processing. "So, my job is to make you a better basketball player. And your job is to teach me to translate the scroll?" I laughed and added, "We both have challenges ahead of us."

Bobby chuckled, raised his eyebrows and raised his fingers together as if he held something. "It takes a small needle to pop that bubble."

"Weak," I jibed, "really weak. — So, when do we start the Hebrew lessons?"

"Professor Sholom is looking forward to doing that with you," Bobby responded. "I wouldn't deprive him of that quest for anything. He's the language master."

"But that could take weeks, Bobby."

"Actually . . . we're talking years to do it well, and months to lay a good foundation."

"So," I combed my fingers through my hair, feeling impatient. "How are we going to investigate a message if I don't know how to translate the message?"

"What does your Dad do for a living?"

"He's a builder."

"Hmmm . . . okay. Here's a question. What does your dad do when certain building materials are not available?"

"He does something else until the . . . materials . . . come. I get it, I get it! We learn to investigate something else."

"You got it . . . We practice with the English version and develop skills in that. One of the basic tools of all time is as simple as an ordinary dictionary."

"What? . . . What could we possibly do with that?"

Do you ever read the bible and you feel like you didn't get anything out of it?"

"All the time."

"Why do you suppose that's the case?"

"Because I'm thinking about other things when I'm reading?"

"That may be the case sometimes. But I'd venture that one likely influence on your wandering mind is that it doesn't have a picture of the meanings of the words. So, when you see or hear those words, a picture doesn't clearly develop. If there's no picture, then the impact isn't maximized. You see what I'm saying?"

"Sure I do. The words I don't *see* are words I won't normally *use*. What you're saying is, if I would study the meanings of just the English words and develop pictures that I understand, what I read would have greater impact."

"That's true to a point. The way different regions and generations use English words and attach definitions to them creates redefining over time. That's called colloquial usage. And etymology studies word development from its origins. When you're looking at a document that is thousands of years old, these are good understandings to consider. Before we work with an ancient language, knowing what to do with the modern language is helpful.

"For example, when you hear the word *apocalypse,* what comes to mind?"[2]

I gave it a brief thought, but it seemed *elementary* as Mister Holmes would say. "That's easy. It's massive global destruction; end of the world stuff."

"Partially correct. That's how we define it today because of the way we've been using it. But that's not the original meaning. A couple thousand years ago, the Greeks used that word to describe something unveiled; a revelation."

"Like the Book of Revelation?"

"That's where the meaning began to change. Because of the *content* of the Revelation, the word became associated with its content rather than its meaning. It doesn't seem like a big deal, but when you get in the habit of finding those things, understanding and accuracy sharpens immensely instead of interpreting scripture through a misplaced paradigm.

"Now, let's go into the professor's workshop. There's an old dictionary in there."

"Bobby, I got one right here on my phone." I had never been in the habit of reading real books. Cavemen and old people did that. "Why bother?"

"It's not the same. I'll show you what I mean."

Bobby touched something on his phone as we headed for the shop and the service door buzzed. Bobby pushed it open. Inside, he pointed to a closet. "Inside that closet is a big ole dictionary. While you bring it out, I'll set up a table."

I went in the closet and couldn't believe what I was seeing. I tried to pick it up. But it was too heavy. So, I got a good grip on the cover and started dragging. The grating sound against the concrete floor was as irritating as grinding two boulders together. "A dolly would work better for this thing," I griped.

"Don't have one. — Sorry."

Meanwhile, Bobby moved a wooden table to the center of the main room where a work light was hanging. He patted the top and said, "We're gonna put 'er there."

We squatted, took a breath, and lifted the bruiser to the table top. The table made a pleading groan under the weight of it. "I feel your pain," I cracked. We laughed. "You really should consider getting the electronic version. Is that cover made out of real stone?"

"Uh, yeah. The front, back and spine is Carrara marble. The pages are real papyrus. It was quite an extraordinary find; very rare. From what I understand, the professor paid a sizable sum for it."

"One-of- a-kind." I was thinking Neanderthal. But it wasn't that old if it was English.

"Yeah, the professor likes vintage stuff."

"I caught that . . . So, what do we do with it? . . . Does it come with instructions?"

"Gee, Caleb. It's pretty straight forward. Do you know the alphabet?"

I was in a mood and couldn't help the digs. "Uh, yeah, I think I'm good. With everything being voice this and voice that, it's a waste of time to learn anymore. In fact, the dictionary on my smart phone is totally voice command *and* response. You sure you don't want to use that?"

"The old ways are good ways, Caleb."

"And heavy ways . . . You'd need a type four warehouse drone to move that thing on a regular basis."

"Uh, I was thinking block and tackle."

"Old ways," I responded.

"Good ways," he countered. "You ready to look up a word?"

"Sure, can you help me lift the cover on this thing and swing it back?"

"You can do it, old chap," Bobby said in a British accent, "nose to the wheel and all that rigmarole."

"I think that's *shoulder* to the wheel, nose to the *grindstone*."

"The world hasn't seen a grindstone in a hundred and fifty years, Caleb."

"I saw one in a blacksmith museum, once. I think they sharpened axes and sickles with it."

Lifting the front cover was a groaner, but I was determined to prove something. — I'm not sure now what it was. "It's definitely heavier than the lid to my old MacBook Pro."

"Come on, man up there. Need some help?" Bobby put a hand out and pulled from the top. We laughed when the cover squeaked.

"I don't understand that," Bobby said with a smirk. "The hinges were oiled fifty years ago. There shouldn't be any resistance."

The cover reached the top of its arch, I lost my grip and it slammed the table top. The table groaned again causing me to wonder, "I don't know if this table is gonna make it, Bobby."

"Pshaw, it's built to last. Let's get down to it . . . Now, when I say the word *redeem*, what comes to mind?"

"Using a gift card to make a purchase?"

"Let me try another approach. When you read the word redeem in the bible, what comes to mind?"

"It has something to do with being saved. It's something Jesus did for you and me . . . Beyond that, nothing much."

"Well then, we have a great place to start. Turn to that word."

I looked at the fragile pages skeptically. I didn't want to tear them. "This would go faster with a search engine, you know."

"I get that. Remember, *the old ways* . . ." Bobby stated with an enthusiastic flare of his right arm.

"Are good ways," I finished with a smirk. Pages turned quickly. "Okay, here's the R's. Racket . . . rainbow . . . rat cheese . . . recover . . . red-blooded . . . redeem . . . Hmm, there's a lot here.

"One . . . to recover ownership of by paying a specified sum.
Two . . . to pay off; like a promissory note.
Three . . . to turn in and receive something in exchange.
Four . . . to fulfill; like a pledge.
Five . . . to convert into cash.
Six . . . to set free; rescue or ransom.
Seven . . . to save from a state of sinfulness and its consequences.
Eight . . . to make up for.
Nine . . . to restore the honor, worth, or reputation of."

Bobby was looking over my shoulder. "Now, let's take each aspect and see which ones line up with what Jesus said and did and what the other apostles wrote."

"One . . . to recover ownership by paying a sum. Corinthians says we were bought with a price.[3] God's ownership of our lives is recovered when we believe in his work on the cross.

"Two . . . to pay off. There's a couple of places in scripture that talks about our debts being forgiven or cancelled out.[4]

"Three . . . To turn in and receive something in exchange. Scripture says we are dead to our old life when we exchange it for our new one in him.[5]

"Four . . . to fulfill, like a pledge. Scripture says Papa gave us Holy Spirit as a pledge, or guarantee, of the inheritance we will receive.[6]

"Five . . . to convert into cash. Hmmm, there's your gift card, Caleb. Many places in scripture speak of us as Papa's treasured possession and also about treasuring him. Yeah, that's a keeper.[7]

"Six…to set free, rescue or ransom. The gospels and the apostle Paul tell us that Jesus' death is a ransom for all of us to be free from sin.[8]

"Seven . . . to save from a state of sinfulness and its consequences. I'd say that one defines us Christians.[9]

"Eight . . . to make up for. Jesus makes up for so much. It would be difficult to make a list of all that he does. In his compassion, he saw us as sheep without a shepherd and brought us into relationship with him. That makes up for a lot of the spiritual blessings that got lost in this fallen world.[10]

"Nine . . . to restore to honor, worth or reputation of. Now there's a big one. Genesis says man was created to be in God's image and enjoy relationship with him. Adam lost that and Jesus restored it.[11] We are now children of God. What an honor that is.

"Caleb, it looks to me that all of them form a large picture of what redemption is. Yet, the smaller pieces carry their own merit. A person could plumb this for hours and come away with a huge treasure. There's so much more. Add to that the historical and Hebrew insights, and you'll have a great understanding to draw from. You won't hear and see that word the same way after today."

"Is that where we get the phrase, 'I see what you're saying?'"

We laughed and Bobby said, "That's funny. Maybe so.

"I mean it, I really see it. Redeem has a big meaning of small meanings and a big picture that can be too big to grasp."

"So, this would be a good place to mention meditation. Meditating on all the parts and considering how they fit together will help you grasp that bigger picture.

"Sometime during the day today or when you go to bed tonight, visualize all these meanings and form pictures of them in your heart. Then visualize what life would be like if you

204

believed them to be true. We'll talk about that at another time."

"You want me to take this monster to bed with me?"

"Oh, certainly not, use your smart phone."

I did a palm plant. Bobby could be unpredictable.

"Let's close the book and call it a day."

I lifted the book leaf and heaved it over the top. The ensuing slam collapsed the table.

We looked at each other and shrugged. "I told you," we said at the same time.

That was a fun lesson. We put the dictionary monster back in its cave and shut the door. Not at my house, I thought. I found a monster e-version when I got home.

The Science in Question[1]

We climbed in the taxi and Bobby gave the driver the address; 221B Baker Street. It was a spontaneous appointment that Bobby made and I was a bit grumped by the last minute change.

"Why couldn't we just do a video link?" I complained. "It would save us energy and time travel."

"You mean travel time, don't you?" Bobby corrected.

When it came to Holmes and Watson, I often wondered if we were breathing the same air. Being around them was thick with mystery. "A slip of the tongue, I think. — Actually, I had my heart set on having some time with Caitlyn this afternoon. I hated to cancel."

Bobby raised a finger. "Ohhhh, now I get it." Then he turned to me and said, "Sounds like she's quite the girl. And probably a good friend to have away from home . . . Sorry, Caleb."

"Do you have a girlfriend, Bobby?"

"Yes, I do. That's why I'm working hard to get done and get home. — Ahhh, that would explain your impatience."

"Don't get me wrong, Bobby, I love being around these guys; I love Sherlock's intensity. And Doctor Watson is the real deal; a people person. But, what's with Mister Holmes insisting on coming to his place?"

"Mister Holmes says," Bobby kicked in a British accent and finished with, "*I deplore electronic communications. It wasn't around in my day.*" He thought a second with a bewildered look; unusual for Bobby. Then he added, "His comment doesn't make sense to me, but I think he prefers an old-fashioned face-to-face way of doing things. He's a bit strange about that. But when it comes to the mastery of asking questions, he *is* the one to seek out. To do so on his terms is not asking too much, is it?"

I looked at Bobby and nodded; assuring him it was okay.

We arrived at the flat, sent off our cabby and knocked on the door. As usual, Mrs. Hudson welcomed us warmly and showed us in with enthusiasm. "It is so wonderful to see young chaps at our place for a change. Most the other gents are older and all stodgified. I can't wait to fix your tea. Can I bring you a crumpet or two?" She managed to put a smile on my face and made me feel like a grandson.

"I'd like that, Mrs. Hudson," I responded.

Mister Sherlock Holmes was seated in his great overstuffed chair in front of the fire with his long legs outstretched. His elbows were on the arms of the chair and his fingertips touched in front of his hawk-like nose. He was unaware to our entry and lost deep in thought.

"Mr. Holmes," Bobby cautiously intruded on his reflections. "What a pleasure to see you again."

Sherlock Holmes blinked and turned his head toward us. Recognition was immediate. He stood and offered his hand.

"Ahh yes . . . gentlemen. I was just reflecting on a current case of mine; very complicated. But I shall have it solved by end of day." While he talked, he moved stacks of books and papers from two chairs and stated, "Please have a seat. Mrs. Hudson will have tea for us straight away."

As we made ourselves comfortable, he probed, "You are here to see me in regard to the science of deduction and analysis. Is that correct?"

"Actually," I rejoined respectfully, "I'd like to learn how to ask good questions about any subject I care to research, particularly the bible."

"Yes, of course, a profound pursuit. Not one I venture into. But I assure you that theory and special knowledge are the immediate steps toward crafting questions in that subject as it is with any other. To receive proper answers, one must ask questions with appropriate depth and direction. Any commoner can dig out a yes or no response and have absolutely nothing to show for it in building a case."

What he said made sense and also made me feel like I said something stupid. I assured myself it wasn't intentional; he had done it before. "Yes," I recovered nervously. "So what you are saying then, is an answer is only as good as the question."

"In the long and short of it all, precisely. Let me illustrate.

"You see, a fool collects every manner of lumber to build with. Soon he is stocked up with assorted useless material as well as the good and cannot lay his hands on what he needs without considerable wasted effort.

"However, a skillful workman is very clever indeed about what he takes in. He then arranges it in its most perfect order for intentional availability. In addition, he will only have what tools are needed to perform his work. A chaotic and untidy workspace leaves a chaotic and untidy mindspace. Neither of which is going to solve anything.

"I presume your father has probably said similar things like that to you, Caleb. Is he not a builder?"

I shouldn't have been shocked, but I was. "How did you know?"

"I am a consulting detective, my dear Caleb, and I suppose the only one in the world. I have a keen ability for observation and for deduction. And the theories I express are very practical although not widely accepted. But I do unravel knots where others fail."

"But, how did you know?"

"From long habit, the train of thoughts ran so swiftly through my mind that I arrived at the conclusion without being conscious of the steps. There *were* such steps, however. The train of reasoning ran, 'Now here is a young fellow with the air and physique of a tradesman, the darker complexion of one who spends time outdoors and dresses commonly in jeans and t-shirt. There is a slight fray at the lower front of his shirt where the buckle from a tool belt has snagged once or twice. And since he is still young, he has clearly worked with his father.' The whole train of thought did not occupy more than a second. I then remarked that your father is a builder and you were astonished."

"It seems simple the way you explain it," I responded.

"If you will, Mr. Holmes," Bobby injected, "what processes would you say are the most effective?"

"The processes, as you request Dr. Kromberg, are a matter of continual practice of basic inquiries and learning to observe."

"I am not a doctor yet, Mr. Holmes."

"You shall be, sir. You have the bearing of success."

"Thank you for your confidence."

"Most certainly. But as I was saying, practice, practice and more practice of the basics. Mastering *who, what, where, when, how and why* in a dozen different contexts is the singular most important beginning. When one answers those points, then observation and deduction fall together like parts of a puzzle."

Mrs. Hudson had entered carrying a tray with tea while Sherlock spoke. She poured and prepared, then handed to each of us. She also made good on bringing us crumpets spread with marmalade. My regret of cancelling Caitlyn faded and Sherlock continued.

"In addition, the careful search for *key* words and *key* phrases are the most enlightening in any correspondence I examine for evidence; very revealing.

"I use these powers in the discipline of criminal and mystery investigation. In the fields of chemistry, anatomy, literature and British law I have achieved some remarkably strong understandings. While in astronomy, politics and philosophy I remain severely feeble. And in still others I languish in mediocrity. Get very keen in the important sciences of your craft, Caleb. And I assure you Bobby, you will gain from this knowledge also."

"I'm sure of that," Bobby responded nibbling a crumpet.

"What you are looking for in your answers may have different details than mine. But the principle observances will be the same. Look for key words and phrases, repetitions and progressions, contrasts and comparisons, causes and effects, motivation and explanation and I am certain, any number more.

"And yet, take a look at my desk and experiment table. It remains cluttered because there is still more work to be done. Even with the most profound inquiries, I have much left on the table to explore, investigate and discover before I draw conclusions. However, at times conclusions must be drawn ready or not. If wrong, do more and try again.

"Now I must say that in the pursuit of visible evidence where a crime has been committed, there is an end of it all in most cases and justice is served. But I am intrigued about this pursuit of yours in spiritual realities. The data is invisible perhaps and difficult to apprehend. What do you seek?"

"The truth of the bible never changes," Bobby stated directly. "But what I believe about truth deepens with revelation, increased faith and inner transformation. Where I have better clarity and broader meaning, I have greater understanding of what I am to believe and how to agree with the transformation that is taking place."

Mister Holmes appeared to be stumped then seemed to find the shelf where Bobby's statement belonged. He put it there and moved on.

"Well then, during the course of your gathering, take time to reflect deeply by way of the principles I have stated and evaluate your findings thoroughly before drawing conclusions. While deliberately blocking out all other distractions, I take as much as several days simply pondering the causes and effects of certain peculiarities and looking at the smaller particles of them as though they were great structures. It is highly effective in my line of work.

"I dare say that in good time, you will have properly sleuthed the knowledge you seek. Therefore, I encourage you to pursue this venture with great passion and never give up.

I thought briefly. And again, it was always amazing how sharp my mind was when he was around. Something in the atmosphere, I think. "So, you use meditation to create questions or make your deductions?"

"It is for both, Caleb. Breaking evidence down to their smallest contributions to the problem at hand are invaluable in seeing the minutiae and rebuilding their solutions into something I can see clearly. It is my opinion though, that meditation is a discipline of the will; blocking out distraction. As I have stated it takes practice and perhaps a willingness to inconvenience the beasts of time and propriety while in process. I have been called rude on many occasions; Doctor Watson being considerably affected. If it is what I must do to get things done, then so be it."

"Gentlemen, I believe we have made considerable progress. When you are ready for more, feel free to return. Now I must be about my business as you must be about yours. I will so enjoy hearing more about your case."

Watch Your Languages

The professor and I were in his office. He had finished his afternoon lecture early and had some time before the end of his day.

"Caleb lad, I've been looking forward to this particular lesson because it speeds me back to the day when I made a deliberate decision to wade into the potentially muddy waters of Hebrew. It wasn't a considerable time afterward, that I included Greek in that pursuit."

"To be honest, Professor, it all sounds like stuffy drudgery."

Professor lowered his eyes and peeked over the top of his glasses and pointed a finger toward me. "You're beginning to sound like a Brit, Caleb. We must work on getting you home." I had to laugh. When in Britainia, it was hard to resist talking like them; there's something fascinating about it. It wasn't just the accent; it was the way they use words.

"Indeed, I understand the drudgery you speak of," he continued. "But even archeologists know we must dig the dirt to get the treasure. Once we find the treasure, we live for nothing else. Allow me to read profound statements from two scholars[1] who lived long before our time." He touched the space bar on his computer and the monitor came to life. "And I quote:

> "When one has read all the various translations, each of which brings out some different shade of meaning from the inexhaustible richness of the Greek text, there still remains a large untranslatable wealth of truth to which only a Greek student has access. The reason for this is that in a translation
>
> which keeps to a minimum of words, that is, where

one English word for instance, is the translation of one Greek word, it is impossible for the translator to bring out all the shades of meaning of the Greek word. It sometimes requires ten or a dozen words to give a well-rounded, full-orbed concept of the Greek word."[2]

"Here is an example of what this man is driving toward."

". . . take the case of the two words translated "love" in I Peter 1:22, the first one meaning "a love that is called out of one's heart by the pleasure one finds in the object loved, and which is nonethical in its nature, an affection, a liking for someone or something," the second, meaning "a love called out of one's heart because of the preciousness of the object loved, and which is sacrificial in its nature, a love conferring blessings upon the object loved." In the first instance, it takes thirty-three words, most of which would appear in a translation that would do justice to the total meaning of the word, to translate the word adequately, and in the second case, thirty words. The single word "love" used to translate these two different Greek words, is a correct rendering and perfectly proper in the ordinary translation. But the English reader would never suspect that there was so much rich material still in the Greek text."[3]

"The differences go even deeper, Caleb, when one includes the brotherly version of love. But you can truly see my point that one love is motivated by pleasure, another motivated by devotion and yet another is motivated by duty. Yet English does not reveal the motive without the addition of stronger language.

My point is not about the different loves, but the need to reinforceme the insufficiencies of the English language.

"Here's another chap; A T Robertson. His books say it this way:

"I have called these volumes, Word Pictures for the obvious reason that language was originally purely pictographic.

"Words have never gotten wholly away from the picture stage. These old Greek words in the New Testament are rich with meaning. They speak to us out of the past and with lively images to those who have eyes to see. It is impossible to translate all of one language into another. Much can be carried over, but not all. Delicate shades of meaning defy the translator. But some of the very words of Jesus we have still as he said: "The words that I have spoken unto you are spirit and are life" (John 6:63). We must never forget that in dealing with the words of Jesus we are dealing with things that have life and breath."[4]

"Pictures have superior impact in comparison to the technicality of words. If a concept or meaning can be seen, it will overshadow the sterility of mere description and last as an indelible impression on the heart. If your heart can see the picture of scripture, you can put it in your own everyday words with powerful consequences. You can insert scripture into everyday conversations with no one knowing. That is why I fell so madly in love with Hebrew. Words are seen in the pictures of human and spiritual events. Hebrew and Greek are glorious languages.

"And when you discover that the Word of God is alive and actively working, even the English words will change your life and the lives of those around you. Although I must add that the same can be said as strongly of the Spirit as it is of the Word. Bobby knows a great deal more about the Spirit than I."

I was stirred, but not convinced. "You have a great passion for these things, Professor. How long did it take you to find that?" I was referring to the idea of how hard it is to stay focused on a new thing day after day. I wasn't up to a long-term commitment.

"I committed to one year. By the end of it, I was hopelessly captivated. I knew it would be a lifetime of treasure hunting for me. It may not be that for you, Caleb. And that's just fine. But if you will, let me challenge you to give it a substantial go. You'll find a niche with it."

"Well, let's get started." My statement sounded uncertain. The professor caught the flavor of it and leaned forward.

"I will endeavor to keep it interesting. Many of my students have called it their favorite classes. It really does grow on you."

And it did. The professor and I had several lessons in England and continued them when I returned home. Professor Sholom booted me out of the nest one day when he stated, "I have given you learning tools to continue without my help. You have learned to learn; a valuable capability under all circumstance. From now on, we will enjoy these times as social pleasures and spiritual treasures."

He was a good spiritual father. He knew how to train me and let me make mistakes with patient guidance. When it was time to cut me loose, he wasn't afraid to bring out the scissors. I miss him considerably; he left this world not long ago. He helped many people over the years. I'm sure his reward is great.

Original languages are my first go-to when I'm hunting for treasure in the word. I'm never disappointed. It provides rich resource for meditation and revelation.

How Do You See It?

Sunday afternoon before dinner, I slammed Bobby at basketball. Three games to zip; it felt good. It would be the last time he let that happen. Below Bobby's mild-mannered exterior is a calculating and patient competitor. He studied my moves and learned to counter them well. It forced me to up my game and be more aggressive; perhaps too aggressive. I felt contentious rather than competitive and Bobby felt my edge. He pointedly mentioned my being a beast on the court was not fun to play against. From then on, I respected what he wanted from our times together. By the time I went home to the states, we were evenly matched, enjoyed our games and good friends.

Mrs. Sholom served a fabulous dinner of lamb roast, veggies and Yorkshire pudding. I pleaded with her to give my mom the Yorkshire recipe next time they talked. She laughed and said she'd be pleased to do so but added that American Yorkshire was not at all like British Yorkshire. The lacking ingredient of the American version was tradition. When I returned home, I discovered what she meant.

After dinner, Bobby and I settled into Professor Sholom's study, rearranged his wing back chairs in front of the hearth and got a fire going. The professor found us there so often that he started calling us hearth buddies. It was his idea of *cozy* and joined us when he could.

After settling in, Bobby got up and pulled a leather-bound book off a shelf and handed it to me. I took it and opened it. The pages were blank, so I looked at him questioning.

Then he sat down and pulled out a pen. "Nice pen," I said. It was comfortably large and red with a turtle shell like design. It had a gold band at the middle.

"This goes with the book," he added.

I took it and gave a closer look. The band was engraved. It said, *Love the Lord with all your heart.*

I smiled and said, "Thank you. — What's on your mind?"

"Something very special to me. Meditation. It has come up in a lot of our conversations. I call meditation the *research and development department* of my spiritual life. It's where I try things on and explore the boundaries of different purviews."

"Could you translate that to English."

"Sure," Bobby responded. "Purview is the extent of my perception, understanding and vision. It includes the realm of where I exist, act and exert influence."

"That sounds like fun." I could also add excitingly adventurous, deeply mysterious and potentially dangerous. But I kept that to myself.

"Remember what Sherlock Holmes said when he wanted a report of all the facts you knew in a case?"

"Let's see if I can impersonate him. I need a hat and pipe." I spotted a pipe on the mantel and looked around for a hat. Minus the hat I sat cross-legged in the chair, pipe in hand. "Let us hear a clear account of what has befallen you. Spare no detail, no matter how trivial you may think it to be."

"Great memory," he said with a wonky smile. "I think the impersonation needs some work . . . But you got the idea. There are things that come to mind that we pass over as trivial, absurd and of little consequence that are actually seeds of creative revelation looking for fertile soil where it can sprout, grow and bloom. Truth and revelation come in seed form. And it's up to us to recognize the seed, wisely cultivate it and grow its potential.

"Several of my father's inventions were the by-product of seed ideas I was given. I was child enough to tell them to my father. He was; and still is; a wise and encouraging teacher. He would listen to them, ask questions, think about it then grow them to bigger ideas. He took me with him through the processes of his meditations where he explored the often-many roads they would take him. Some were dead end; and he expected that. Even when he found a train of thought that had merit, he would still try others.

"It was like following a wandering stream; not knowing where it would go. But there would be an end one way or another. I learned a lot from those days and still use those lessons for scientific purposes. I have refined others for scripture studies and sorting out spiritual realities."

"So, you have rules for meditation." Builders like rules and methods; it's how my father trained me to build things.

"No. I have scripture that *shows* me various forms of meditation. The first mention of it is in Genesis.[1] Isaac went out to meditate in the field toward evening; and he lifted up his eyes and looked, and behold, camels were coming.

"In the Hebrew text, there is a lot more said than in the English. The word used for meditation gives a broad understanding of what he could have been doing. He could have been praying, he might have been complaining, he possibly repeated thoughts he was entertaining. He was likely talking to himself or to God out loud. At the core of it, he was opening up his heart as deeply as possible and being real. And given the text, God was listening to whatever it was.

"What follows gives us a hint. While he was meditating, something got his attention. It caused him to consider, change his perspective and look around. The answer to what was on his mind was in front of him. By the end of the chapter, he and Rebekah were married and he was deeply comforted."

"Sounds like a 'they lived happily ever after' storybook ending.

I must be missing the point. What is it?"

"Meditation opened Isaac's eyes to what he couldn't see. His sight was limited to what was in front of him. We aren't told what he experienced. But we know there was a shift. *Lifting up his eyes* is a Hebrew idiom about trust. Somehow, he found trust or faith or belief; whatever it is called in the moment; the answer to the cry of his heart followed.

"King David meditated to not only commune with his heart,[2] but also to find the right words for the songs he wrote. Meditation was a part of David's creative process, gave God access to his inner life and occupied him with remembering the things of God.[3]

"We can often look truth in the face and not see it. It's just words. Many times, I have looked at scripture and asked, 'What would my life look like if I actually believed it?' Through meditation I saw the different views of my faith and challenged what and if I believed. Sometimes there would be immediate breakthrough, and sometimes more process. But when I could see the objective, I knew I was on the right path."

"That's a lot to chew on, Bobby."

"That's a lot of the idea of meditation. It's chewing on something with careful, undistracted thought and filling the heart with it. The notebook and pen are for writing meditations down in whatever form they come. Complete ideas, or larger pictures, have come from bringing together smaller pictures and partial ideas. It's a process and a discipline and it takes practice.

"Carry that notebook with you and . . ."

I had to interrupt, "Can I use my smart-phone?" It was a dig in remembrance of our dictionary talk.

Bobby rolled his eyes and said, "Of course. The idea is to write down details and thoughts that come to you. No matter how trivial you think they may be, record them before you forget them. Next time you're alone with the Lord, ask for more revelation and meditate on them."

Since that talk with Bobby, I have found other scriptures that reinforce what he said and add other avenues for meditation. My favorite is this:

So keep your thoughts continually fixed on all that is authentic and real, honorable and admirable, beautiful and respectful, pure and holy, merciful and kind. And fasten your thoughts on every glorious work of God, praising him always.[4]

What I say is a reflection of my inner life. Jesus put it this way, ". . . what comes out of your mouth reveals the core of your heart."[5] And I am responsible for my heart. I need to watch over my thoughts, my will, my discernment and my affections. What do I allow to be there?[6]

So, I add my agreement to King David's voice, *may the words of my mouth, my meditation-thoughts, and every movement of my heart be always pure and pleasing, acceptable before your eyes, my only Redeemer, my Protector-God.*[7]

Unlocking the Golden Scroll well, gives Papa God the opportunity to unlock us so he can create in us a heart of gold and a renewed mind. It's an exchange, a very incredible exchange.

Forming the Scroll

Author's note: This excerpt from Caleb's journal doesn't fit in a how-to category. It had the potential to be part of the story, but seemed out of place anywhere in the flow of it. It wasn't a nuts and bolts conversation about Unlocking the Golden Scroll. It stood alone, interesting and informative about the scroll. It held my attention, and I know it will yours.

* * * * * * * * *

Bobby and I had an unusual talk. It was speculative but made sense somehow. But I knew I might forget because of the overcrowding of my mind with a constant flow of new memories. In light of how my life had catapulted me through so many adventures, it was possible. Regardless of my capacity and what I think of it, before I returned from England it was a high priority entry in my journal.

After a foggy afternoon of basketball, Bobby and I fell into a random conversation about science and the realms of space. We touched on the golden scroll, wondering how it was formed, and the conversation took off from there.

Bobby ran through facts about it that deserved consideration. "Everything about it is gold in one form or another. The parchment is gold, and yet it is a fabric, but woven fine enough to write on. And the ink is a gold alloy of some kind. Yet its makeup could not have been made on earth. There is no historical or scientific data to verify that anything like it ever existed naturally in the earthly realm."

My response was, "I have heard of black gold in the Dakotas, but this must be different. How could black ink be made from gold?"

"It could actually be an alloy or mixture of cobalt and gold that gives it the black color," Bobby stated. "To use it as an ink, would mean the liquid was molten at the time of its writing."

I pictured a hand with a gigantic quill pen dipping into a volcanic ink jar and writing furiously before it cooled. It was humorous to imagine, but made it easy to grasp. "The rock that surrounded the original cylinder was black. I saved most of it. We could have it checked out."

"If the makeup of that rock is similar to the makeup of the ink in the scroll, Caleb, it would imply that the rock, the cylinder and the scroll were created at the same time."

My capacity to apprehend that scenario hit a wall. "I think you're losing me. How could that happen?"

"The circumstances would be unique to its creation, with no earthly similarity; it would have been crafted without precedent. It would be impossible in Earth's natural atmosphere. And to scientifically grasp an environment where its formation could happen, is speculative at best.

"There is a celestial origin theory about gold and its presence on earth. In short, it implies that all gold that was present on earth during the molten formation of the planet sank to the core as it cooled. And any gold present on the surface now is extraterrestrial and came to earth during the Late Heavy Bombardment.

"Out in the cosmos, gold is formed in the collision of neutron stars and the resulting kilonova. Or, from the supernova of an exploding star."

"Decades ago, in 2017, there was a recorded cosmic event that was believed to be the merger of two neutron stars in the Hydra constellation. The gamma-ray bursts and gravitational waves were recorded and the light show eleven hours later was observable. — I wish I could have seen that one."

"Was the collision you saw with your dad something like

that?"

"Those bodies were planetoid and asteroid in nature. Given more precise data, it is possible that collision and the scroll may have the same origins. The amount of energy in a neutron star collision is beyond our ability to calculate and what it sets in motion is unfathomable.

"Here's the big thing, Caleb. That scroll would have been created and written in the extreme energy of that kilonova. Then put in the cylinder and wrapped in the rock as it cooled."

"That just wonks my mind, Bobby. How long would that event last?"

"About two seconds."

"That's not possible."

"Not in the natural. But where time and natural physics are not components of the equation, anything can happen . . . Hey, here's a question for you, Caleb. When did time begin?"

"Time began when I got out of bed this morning . . . Gosh Bobby, how do I know when time began? How about asking a small question?"

"Okay. Do you read your bible?"

"I've read the gospels a couple of times. But I'm just starting as a bible reader."

As Bobby tapped his smart phone he said, "You will be." A text from the bible appeared on a nearby screen. He tapped it again and a page from the first chapter of the book of Genesis displayed.

"Start at verse fourteen and read through nineteen."

"Okay . . . And God said, "Let there be bright lights to shine in space to bathe the earth with their light. Let them serve as signs to separate the day from night, and signify the days, seasons and years." And so it happened. God made two great lights: the brighter light to rule the day and the lesser light to rule the night. He also set the tapestry of shining stars and set them all in the sky to illuminate the earth, to rule over the day and to rule over the night, and to separate the light from darkness. God loved what he saw, for it was beautiful. Evening gave way to morning — day four."

Bobby smiled and asked, "If there were no sun or the moon's reflection of the sun, and there were no stars during the first three days of creation, there was no sunrise or sunset."

Bobby gave me enough pause to let that soak in. "Why do I get the feeling that my mind is going to spin? There couldn't be an evening and morning as we know it without a sun."

"As we know it, that is scientific fact, Caleb. No arguments there."

Here was my clear point of brilliance. "That means time probably wasn't ticking in the same way it is today until the fourth day of creation."

"There again, no disagreement with that."

"If 'Let there be light,' of the first day of creation separated light from darkness, how is it different from the night and day of the fourth day? And how long were the first three days if there was no time?"

"We aren't told, Caleb. But we know it was outside of whatever time we use today. Before you go off the deep end, I guarantee you can't wrap your head around it. You'll blow a circuit trying to figure it out."

My annoyance ramped up a couple notches. "Come on, you can't just leave me hanging like that."

"The very best I can do is use it, however imperfectly, to explain dinosaurs, the existence of fossil fuels and other assorted minor issues. According to the Hebrew text, light was created; the word is *or* in Hebrew; on the first day, but no bright lights or stars; *maor*; until the fourth day. It's just impossible to connect all the dots and draw any conclusion that can be explained precisely. I've tried and all I can say is God didn't tell us."

"That sucks. Why would he do that?"

"I can only suppose that if we had creation figured out, it wouldn't take faith to know the creator, or understand that what he's looking to get from us is a love for him that is more important than scientific knowledge or systematic reasoning. It's a voluntary love that trusts Father God without solid evidence."[1]

With that, I stood up. "Great! So what you're saying is . . . this scroll was created outside of time and made of things impossible to recreate on earth."

"Probably."

"And what you're also saying is that there is some importance about this scroll being written in Hebrew."

"Either there's something in it or about it that we need to know, or it's pointing to something we don't yet see; some mystery."

Caleb smiled. "He's concealing something in it we need to find."

"There are parts of this adventure that may not be all that mysterious, Caleb. What we need to intimately know is the truth. Consider this idea: emotions are a very valid part of our lives. Yet if we don't know the truth of who we are and who Jesus and our Father is, we can be ruled or deceived by what we feel. There are religious cults that trick people into feeling good about lies by having them pray for a feeling that isn't based in the truth of scripture. Then they go off in pursuit of another god; deceived by feeling instead of believing the truth."

"Then why have emotions if we can't trust them?"

"Emotions synchronized with spirit and truth is good.

"The book of Colossians[2] tells us to be richly, generously and abundantly alive with the words of Jesus and filled with spiritual songs and gratefulness. The root form of the Greek word implies that we are wealthy if we live that way. That fullness will keep us on the power path of life and living above unnecessary struggles."

I thought about it for a minute. "If all I need is to be made alive with the life of Jesus, then what is this celestial scroll all about?"

"Well Sherlock, that's the nature of a mystery, isn't it?"

The Backstory

The formation of this allegory birthed in late 2017. Reading Randy Ingermanson's book, *How to Write a Novel Using the Snowflake Method,* was the first nugget. He used a story to portray his method. Revolutionary to my literary senses, it was provocative. Yet, it offered another device for my creative tool crib.

Later, someone mentioned their struggle with the enjoyment of studying the bible consistently. That statement triggered a flood of comical ideas. It challenged me to create a story that would be fun to read, challenge increasing faith and incorporate personal components of scriptural treasure hunting that I use.

So, in 2018 I stopped work on another project to write the rough draft of this book. When the rough was done, I finished The Revolution. Afterwards, a second wave of storyline expanded the overall depth of this project. I had a lot of fun pulling it together.

Some characters and location spin off the Renascence Series (alternate spelling intentional). Grandma Rachel was a toddler in The Revolution (Book 2). Richard and Bobby Kromberg are her progeny. The curious story of talking goats is presented in The Ruction (Book 1) So, the setting of this story is three generations removed from the original and for the most part, unrelated.

Reading the bible in any English version is fruitful. It will renew our minds, heal our lives in any variety of ways and give us resource to share with others. After reading several versions from cover to cover multiple times, I was still hungry for more. I went after Hebrew just like Professor Sholom, and found a lifetime passion. Greek followed and I became a treasure hunter. As for the components of treasure hunting the Word given here, Holy Spirit developed them in me over the years of my journey.

Several years ago my professor, Dr. John Amstutz, introduced me to the fine art of observation and deduction; forming questions with the purpose of getting useful answers. When I was forming the storyline of this book, I went back to the resources of that time and found it difficult to create a story around the method I learned. That's when Sir Arthur Conan Doyle stepped out of the shadows and rudely demanded my attention. With a subtle inference of time travel and reading a lot of Doyle's work, Holmes, Watson and England were assimilated into the story instead. The result is cheeky, but gets the job done.

"One can *know* the Word, and still not *believe* it." That was a confrontation from Ray Leight in his work with "Who Do you Think You Are?" It's a confrontation that demands a response to look at the scriptures we know and see if we truly believe them; about God, ourselves and about the authority we have. Ray and I had several lunches together while we discussed the depth of problems that arise when we don't believe what we know to be true. Those conversations also included the immeasurable freedom and blessings that come when we do believe it. Perhaps that is why we are called *believers*.

God can do *anything*. This book expands traditional boundaries way beyond usual expectations; even to hyperbole or exaggeration; of what can happen through faith and trust. Although there's a good chance we won't be called on to recreate the moon, none of what is given in this book is impossible for God and for his people.

Unlocking the Golden Scroll is *not* a complete pictorial of the Kingdom of God. The focus of this story is to reveal the extraordinary living treasure that is the Word of God (the bible), and how to unlock its wealth. Plus, I expose readers to aspects of the makeover life that comes with being a disciple of Jesus. There's a lot of action and adventure scenes in the Christian life. And there are trials. Their purposes are to unlock the gold in us and display us as representations of the living and loving God.

Jesus is the Word made flesh. And so it is meant to be with us; we become the Word by way of Holy Spirit living inside us and we aligning with his Word. It's rarely comfortable and often demands the surrender of our old nature to allow a new nature to form. Our lives can be lived out naturally ordinary. But God's intention is that we live supernaturally extraordinary. It can only be done his way. Situations of trial that develop character in Caleb and Bobby were included for a very good reason; the hunger to go deeper in God will lead us to heart changes that make room for his presence and his word.

Here's a quote written on the back page of Smith Wigglesworth's pocket bible that reaches back to another generation.[1]

> *"Never compare this book with other books. Comparisons are dangerous. Never think or say that this book contains the Word of God. IT IS the Word of God. It is supernatural in origin, eternal in duration, inexpressible in value. Infinite in scope, regenerative in power, infallible in authority, universal in interest, personal in application, inspired in totality. Read it through. Write it down. Pray it in. Work it out. And pass it on. It IS the Word of GOD."*

God's Word is constantly revealing because we are continually being changed by it. As we learn to handle it well,[2] he entrusts us with more revelation. It's a stewardship we should take seriously. These two verses from Psalm 119 are reminders to me to guard it with love.

Psalm 119:162 says: *"Your promises are the source of my bubbling joy; the revelation of your word thrills me like one who has discovered hidden treasure."*

Also verse 169: *"Lord, listen to my prayer. It's like a sacrifice I bring to you; I must have more revelation of your word."*

From the inside out, I want to be a habitation for God in Spirit and in truth. I hope you will too.

My prayer and blessing for anyone who has read this book: May a fire be ignited within you to hunger and thirst for his Spirit and his Word. May you find his presence your true dwelling place.

If this book has stirred something in you, I'd love to hear from you.

Email me at: friends@creativestirrings.org

Endnotes

Unless otherwise specified, all scripture quotations are from The Passion Translation (TPT).

Chapter one

1. Genesis 1:14. In Hebrew, a day (yom) has a vastly larger meaning than a 24-hour span. It can be eons (the longest division of geologic time) and epochs. An epoch marks the characteristics of a *particular* period of history or instant in time. Its use is in reference to daily life, astronomy, physics and paleontology.

A season (moed) marks the annual cycles, but also includes a specially designated appointed time not necessarily related to a yearly or lunar cycle.

2. Jeremiah 33:3. "Call to me and I will answer you and show you great and mighty things, fenced in and hidden, which you do not know (do not distinguish and recognize, have knowledge of and understand). [Amplified Bible]

3. One astronomical unit is roughly the distance from earth to the sun, and approximately equal to 93 million miles (150 kilometers)

Chapter three
1. Luke 2:41-52
2. Psalm 37:23

Chapter fifteen
1. Psalm 119:162
2. Proverbs 25:2
3. Romans 8:17

Chapter sixteen
1. Chapters sixteen and seventeen are written in the traditional Sir Arthur Conan Doyle style of his Sherlock Holmes stories; Doctor Watson is narrating in first person. The scene is literarily daring. It meant pulling the characters through a two-hundred-year

worm hole and creating the subtle appearance of time travel.

Chapter twenty-three
1. See Part 2, "About Definitions"
2. Mark 13:32-33
3. Revelation 20:1-8
4. Mark 13:31, Isaiah 34:4, Revelation 6:14
5. Romans 8:28-31

Chapter twenty-six
1. J.R.R. Tolkien, The Riddle of Strider, The Lord of the Rings; The Fellowship of the Rings.

Chapter thirty
1. Creative liberty is taken to picture prophetic expression from Revelation, chapter 8.

Chapter thirty-one
1. Isaiah 24:17-20
2. Revelation 8:10-11
3. Matthew 17:20-21
4. Luke 17:6
5. John 15:7-8
6. John 14:12-13
7. John 16:16 [emphasis added]
8. Matthew 6:1
9. Luke 11:10
10. Matthew 18:19-20
11. Joshua 10:12-13
12 Ephesians 4:13
13. 1 John 4:17
14. Ephesians 1:20-2:6

Chapter thirty-three
1. John 15:4b
2. John 15:18-19
3. 1 Corinthians 2:9
4. John 15:18-19
5. Their history is told in The Renascence Series, beginning with The Ruction.

Part Two

Peeling the Layers

1. Catalogue of English Bible Translations, Wm. J Chamberlin, 1991
2. Colossians 3:16

The Defining Factors

1. Proverbs 25:2
2. Mention in Chapter 23
3. 1 Corinthians 6:19-20, 7:22-23, Colossians 1:19-20
4. Matthew 6:12, 18:23-27, Colossians 2:13-14
5. Romans 6, 7 and 8
6. 2 Corinthians 5:4-5, Ephesians 1:13-14
7. Exodus 19:4-6, Deuteronomy 7:6-8, Isaiah 55:1-3, Matthew 6:19-21, 2 Corinthians 4:6-7, Colossians 2:1-3
8. Matthew 20:28, Mark 10:45, 1 Timothy 2:6, Galatians 5:1
9. Isaiah 43:25, 44:22, Acts 3:19-21, Matthew 26:26-29
   Romans 4:1-8, Ephesians 1:3-14
10. Matthew 9:36, Mark 6:34, John 10:11, 1 Peter 5:4, Romans 8,
    Ephesians 1:3-12
11. Romans 8, Galatians 3:29, 4:7, James 2:5

The Science In Question

1. A similar scene would be found in "A Study in Scarlet" by Sir Arthur Conan Doyle,
   first published in 1887. Public domain.

Watch Your Languages

1. Kenneth Wuest and A. T. Robertson
2 and 3. Wuest's Word Studies from the Greek New Testament
4. Robertson's Word Pictures in the Greek New Testament

How Do You see It?
1. Genesis 24:63, New American Standard
2. Psalm 77:6
3. Psalm 5:1, 104:34, 119:15 (and so much more)
4. Philippians 4:8
5. Matthew 15:18, Luke 6:45
6. Proverbs 4:23
7. Psalm 19:14

Forming the Scroll
1. Hebrews 11:1
2. See Colossians 3:16-17

The Backstory
1. Thanks to Bill Johnson for sharing with the rest of the family.
2. 2 Timothy 2:15

www.ingramcontent.com/pod-product-compliance
Lightning Source LLC
Chambersburg PA
CBHW061032120726
47910CB00006B/2212